BARROW & BONE

AN AUTUMN ANTHOLOGY OF CELTIC and GERMANIC MYTHS

REBECCA F. KENNEY

First Edition: September 2022

Kenney, Rebecca F.
Barrow and Bone / by Rebecca F. Kenney—First edition.

CONTENTS

**Adult content,
child abuse, child labor/slavery,
mention of child death,
violence, gore, cruelty,
body horror, monsters**

1

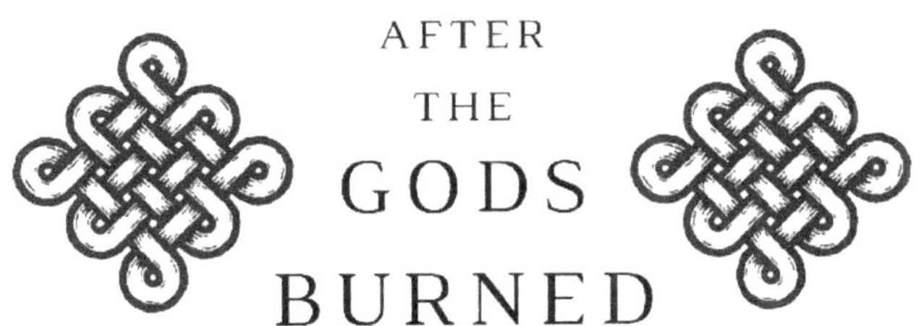

The People of Danu were gone.

A good thing, some said. The immortal god-race had lorded it over the humans of the Green Isle long enough.

Well, not immortal, after all. They burned easily enough, once they had been drugged and knotted with druid charms to bind their magic.

A year ago, Mairead had witnessed a burning—a gigantic wicker figure, stuffed with the bodies of the Tuatha dé Danann and their allies. Long graceful limbs draped from the effigy's eyeholes and armpits. Beautiful faces, dark and pale alike, showed between the bundles of sticks—faces smooth in drugged sleep, some with faint frowns as they slowly woke to their condition. Too late, too late, for the fire was already gobbling up the legs of the effigy, clambering higher, faster, cackling and crunching. Catching on skin, drying it up into crispy flakes, melting the flesh and sizzling the blood, eating down, down to the bone.

Druids stood in a carefully spaced ring around the effigy, chanting a sonorous song. The villagers around Mairead cheered now and then—soft at first, then louder, emboldened by each other's voices.

"It's about time," said one man.

"Truth," said another. "I'd rather be serf to a lord who shares our race, and our mortal years. Not these unnatural devils with their Otherworldly powers. The druids, now—they have magic, but it's *honest* magic, of earth and blood and bone. They're human, like us."

"Drive out the People, and the other Fae will leave as well," a third interjected. "I've had enough of those pooka shapeshifters, and the selkies clogging up our rivers, and the pixies wandering about the woods. Aimless they are, shiftless no-good fell creatures. We'd best be rid of them all."

Mairead felt vaguely unsettled. Before Da died, he'd told her to respect the People. "They keep us safe," he'd said. "They move the winds and water for us, keep the earth fertile, hold back the Unseelie—the *amadan dubh*, bringer of madness, and the *alp-luachra*, belly-eater. Honor the Tuatha dé Danann, Mairead my love, and they will protect you."

Mairead had been eighteen when he died. A year later, the People were burning—burning, or sailing across the Western Sea to escape the mobs that hunted them. One more year beyond that, and Mairead was a woman of twenty, standing in the center of a bedraggled field, nigh to weeping over the sickly stalks of grain, wondering if perhaps Da had been right. Life seemed no better under the rule of the druids and their harsh queen. In fact, Mairead was willing to bet her Da's dying farm that life was worse than ever.

The sun crushed her with a fierce, unrelenting heat. Her head thrummed with dull pain, and her heart jittered uncertainly beneath her ribs. She had been working the fields for too long without water and without rest.

She let the hoe fall from her hand and staggered toward a towering oak tree. Its leaves were a dull brown from the sun's glare and the lack of rain, but they still provided some shade. Mairead collapsed on the grass beneath the tree, her stomach twisting at the brittle crunch of the grass. Everything was dry. Everything was dying.

Harvest should be a joyful time—gardens surging with bounty, fields rippling with grain. Not this skeletal field, these papery stalks.

She lay on her back, staring up at the withering tree. With her left arm she reached out, until her palm contacted the trunk. Coarse as the wood of her father's coffin. Dusty as the bones within.

Tears pooled in Mairead's eyes.

"I am sorry," she whispered. Maybe she was speaking to the tree, or to the fields. Maybe she was praying to the People, proud and powerful. Gods destroyed by human hate.

She leaned on one elbow long enough to sip water from the flask at her belt. Then she collapsed again, her spine seamed to the earth. She would rest here for a little while, and then go back to work. If she could not make the farm support her, she must marry. She was not beautiful—raw-boned from hunger, lacking the plumpness of prosperity. Her eyes were dark and luminous, but sunken. Her hair was no glory, either, plaited into a long thin braid at her back. She was an assembly of bones and desperation, her smile too sharp and earnest. And her land was no great acquisition, either.

Choices circled round and round in her head—precious few of them, and none she liked. Slowly the circles merged into dark, clouded dreams.

She startled awake, into a dusk of dull red light and gray shadow. Her throat felt sore and scratchy—she must have been sleeping with her mouth open. Quickly she swigged a little more water. It helped, but did not sate the roaring hunger in her stomach.

Cursing herself for her slothfulness in sleeping away the day, she trudged back across the fields, to the tiny cottage she and Da had shared. Ma had been there too, until Mairead was ten.

Saoirse, the midwife who lived two farms over, had given Mairead some advice after Da passed. "Welcome the memories into your heart," she had said. "Treat them as old friends, and they will be kind to you. Remember the good times, and it will soften the loss."

Mairead had tried to embrace the memories as old friends—but they were friends with sharp nails that slit the coating of her heart and pierced deep into the pounding muscle. Sometimes she embraced them so tightly she could hardly breathe.

In a way she was lucky to have this undesirable parcel of land, and to be plain as she was. It meant that no one tried to take her or her property by force. The nearby farms were owned by good families who looked out for each other—families who had brought her soup and bread after Da passed. Families who stood arm in arm while the wicker figures burned, while the beautiful gods dissolved into smoke and ash.

Mairead stumbled into the cottage, exhausted despite her hours of sleep. Her hands trembled so harshly with hunger that she could barely light a candle. She wolfed down a hunk of bread and stared desperately at the rest of the loaf. She should save it, but she was so hollow inside. So very hungry.

At last she tore away another piece. She offered a bit of it to the cat, Gadaí, but the animal only sniffed it and stalked primly past her. Gadaí was a good mouser and rat-catcher, and probably had a full belly—something Mairead could only dream of these days.

Caught in a ravenous compulsion, Mairead ripped into the rest of the loaf. Each bite was like a balm, a blessed relief. She swallowed down the last morsel and sighed. The ache inside her was finally gone, her belly sated.

She crept into bed and clawed the thin blankets over her. Gadaí settled over her feet, a pleasant weight of fur and warmth.

In the night Mairead jerked awake, gasping, clutching her stomach. A cavern of gut-wrenching hunger had opened up inside her. She lunged from the bed, lurching over to the cupboard and tearing out its contents—her sole remaining loaf, a piece of hard cheese she'd been saving for a treat, and some skeletal carrots.

Mairead gnawed a carrot, her panic rising as she stared at her tiny store of food. Hungry, so hungry. But she must not eat it all. She must not. If she gobbled it all now, she would starve later.

Just this one carrot.

And then another.

One more, and the cheese as well. Half the bread. The whole loaf. And the rind of the cheese.

That was all she had, and it was enough. The roar of her hunger had quieted.

She slipped under the blankets again, a frown tightening her forehead. She had been hungry before, many times, but never like this. Never this all-consuming, mind-gnawing, stomach-churning *need*. Perhaps she was ill. She had no time to be ill, not with all the work to be done. Not when her cupboard was bare of everything—when she'd devoured it all—

She rolled over, burying her face in the thin pillow, and sobbed herself to sleep.

Mairead woke again at her usual rising time, in the dim quiet just before dawn. She swung her legs out of the bed, wavered, and nearly toppled headlong to the floor. Her head swam. Every muscle of her body felt loose and limp. Hunger clawed her insides again.

Her stomach growled, louder than she had ever heard it growl before. And then it— flipped. Twisted. She felt the slosh of liquid, the lurch of a movement that she had not initiated.

Mairead clapped a hand over her middle. Her throat constricted, barely enough space for air to squeeze through.

She had imagined it of course. Bellies did not move in that way on their own—unless—

Unless perhaps she was with child. She had seen pregnant women's bellies sway and stretch as their infant moved inside them.

Not possible. Her bleeding had been less than a week ago, not enough time for a child to grow—and she had been with no man, ever. Unless someone had come to her when she was asleep, and done the deed quietly—but no. That did not seem likely, or possible. She was a light sleeper, and would have woken to an intruder. Her door had a solid latch, as did her shutters, and the cat lay always upon Mairead's feet at night. Gadaí would have squalled like a banshee had anyone tried to disturb her resting place.

Besides, Mairead's hunger resided in the center of her torso, right under her ribs, and she thought that a woman's birthing area was lower down, though she had never seen a sketch of the internal organs.

One person might know—the midwife, Saoirse, who served as counselor and physician to everyone in the area, as well as a caregiver to women with child.

Still shaking, Mairead managed to wash up and straighten her clothes. She did not bother replaiting her messy braid.

Panic drove her from the cottage. Her ankles wobbled, twisting occasionally as she hurried up the deeply rutted road. The air was chill, but not as damp as it should be on an autumn morning. Drought, the terror of farmers and all living things, had stolen the dew itself.

The hair on Mairead's arms lifted against the hiss of the cold air. She had forgotten to bring a shawl.

Her way was haunted by lichen-laced trees, crooked fences, and the broken lines of the hedgerows. Only the low, winding walls of chiseled stone offered her any comfort. They were sturdy and solid, an ever-present surety in this part of the world.

She climbed a stile and crossed a field to shorten her journey to Saoirse's house. The hunger inside her had transformed into a gnarled pit of pain, so fierce she actually considered gathering a handful of grass and gnawing it while she walked. But she resisted, because she could not show up at the door chewing a mouthful of grass. They would think her mad.

Again a lurch in her gut. Something—moving—inside her. Mairead whimpered and ran, as if the frantic thump of her feet on the turf could settle the skittering pace of her heart. As if she could outrun the thing, the *Thing* that was inside her.

She crashed against Saoirse's door, sobbing and pleading, thumping with fists weak from hunger. The door opened almost at once, and Saoirse's husband, who was used to occasional visits by frantic women, gripped her upper arm and drew her inside.

"Hush, now," he said. "The little ones be sleepin' still. You'll be here to see Saoirse, eh? She's out in the privy, be right with ye. Sit ye down, love. It'll all be right, ye'll see."

Mairead collapsed onto the bench he indicated. "Do you—do you have anything to eat?" She scarcely managed the words through the thickness of her pride. But the hunger was so savage, so all-consuming—she thought her body might begin to devour its own organs if she did not eat something soon.

"Sure, sure." Saoirse's husband glanced around, rubbing the back of his neck with a meaty hand. "I can get ye a bit o' bread."

"Please. Anything."

"All right then, all right." He shuffled to a wooden bin and took out a loaf, cutting a generous slice for Mairead. She couldn't eat it fast enough.

"Starvin', are ye?"

"Something like that," whispered Mairead.

Saoirse bustled in then, tying on her apron. Her eyebrows lifted at the sight of Mairead. "Up early, are we, my dear? Need something?"

"She's in a bad way, love," said her husband. "I got to tend to the beasts. Give her some care, eh?"

"I'll do that." Saoirse approached, inspecting Mairead. "What is it then, dearie? Got yourself in a tangle?"

Between half-sobs, Mairead described her condition. Saoirse's frown deepened the longer she talked.

"Lie down on the bench," said the midwife. "I want a look at your stomach."

Mairead lay back. At the movement, something tugged at her insides, a sickening sensation.

Saoirse lifted Mairead's skirts, bunching them all the way up to her rib cage. "Hold these a moment." Her practiced fingers pressed along Mairead's abdomen and sides, then traveled over her stomach, under her ribcage.

The thing inside Mairead's body quivered.

Saoirse's fingers froze. Then she poked a little deeper in that spot.

Mairead's belly surged and twisted. She looked down, between her breasts, over the bunched skirts, and saw her own skin undulating with the movement of something that was Not Her.

She screamed.

Saoirse clapped a hand over Mairead's mouth. "Hush, now, hush. Stop, Mairead. Stop it. I know what it is. I can help you, do you hear me? I can help you."

Mairead quieted, tears streaming across her temples. She nodded, and Saoirse removed her hand. "It's not a baby," she said. "But you have a creature inside you, dear, and it's not pleasant. I've seen a case like this once, when my mother was teaching me the midwife's trade. A man, with his belly distended, rippling as something moved within him. He was starving, eating everything in sight, but he stayed skin and bones while his belly grew. It was the beastie inside, you see, that was eating every bit of food in his stomach. His body couldn't get much of it. It was all going to the monster."

Mairead whimpered. "Please, please—"

"At that time it was an easy thing to cure," said Saoirse. "My mother took him to one of the People, and they used magic to suck the thing out of him. They walked the land afterward, too, to root out any more of the horrible creatures."

"What is it?" whispered Mairead.

"*Alp-luachra*," replied Saoirse. "Belly-eater, gut-splitter. It crawls down a human's throat while they're sleeping, curls up in the belly. The bile doesn't bother them—they got skin as can handle it. They eat most of what goes down your gullet, and they always want more. They grow and grow, until they get so big the human's skin stretches and then they burst out, fully mature, with a brood of little monsters ready to be birthed. You're lucky, dear. Yours is a small one so far, barely large enough to make a lump." She patted Mairead's belly, and the *alp-luachra* twitched in response.

Mairead thought perhaps she might begin to scream, and once she started she might shriek horribly, on and on, forever. She would not be able to stuff the panic back in again. She scarcely dared open her lips to speak. "You said you could help me."

"As I said, when the Tuatha dé Danann lived throughout this region, it would have been easy. They could have cured you with magic."

Mairead choked on the memory of delicate features vanishing in a cloud of smoke, of skin seared and bubbling.

Their magic.

They could have cured you.

"There is one other thing we can try," said the midwife. "An old remedy, and not a sure thing."

"My other choice is death," said Mairead. "I will try anything."

"You're going to need a lot of salty food—salt beef, or salt fish," said Saoirse. "Cashel up in the grove has a store of it—he's had good luck fishing and hunting even when others haven't. Go to him, and barter for a supply of salted food. Take the food to the river and eat it—all of it. Do not—and this is very important—do not drink even one drop of water. The *alp-luachra* thrive in moisture. They need water to live. You keep eating the salty food until you think you will be sick, and then lie down beside the water with your mouth open. You will crave water—you may nearly die of thirst. Do not drink. When the *alp-luachra* is desperate enough, it will crawl out of you and go to the water."

Mairead stared. "That is the cure? The only way?"

"Yes."

"Can I not vomit it out?"

"It must leave of its own accord. If you try to expunge it another way, it will sink its spines into your stomach and hold fast, and you will die all the sooner. You must try the salt purge, Mairead."

"But will it work?"

Saoirse shrugged. "Who knows? I hope for your sake that it does. You should hurry to Cashel's place. Tell no one what has infected you, or you may find yourself burning alive on a druid pyre. And here—take this." She handed over the remainder of the loaf from the bin. "May Eriu smile upon you."

It was a Fae blessing, one spoken only by the allies of the Tuatha dé Danann. Saoirse was putting her very life into Mairead's hands by speaking it.

The midwife gave her a sympathetic grimace and ushered her out the door of the house. "Go, quickly, my dear! And be sure to tell me if it works!"

A dark horror gripped Mairead's mind as she staggered along the lane toward the forest. It was a long walk to the grove near the river where Cashel lived. She had been there twice with Da, to trade vegetables for fish, so she knew the way; but she could not imagine walking that path while carrying a monster in her belly. Not when all she wanted to do was to curl in on herself and hide in a hollow just big enough for her body, and submerge her consciousness in the aching blackness of terror.

Had it not been enough? The loss of Ma, and Da—the massacres of the Tuatha dé Danann, the drought, the agonized spasms of a land transitioning from its former magic to— nothing.

Had she not endured enough?

She remembered seeing the Tuatha dé Danann from time to time when she was younger, before the tide turned against them and they became more secretive and scarce. She recalled their height and grace, their crisp beauty. Some were stern and rigid, barely acknowledging her and Da—others smiled and nodded, accepting the respectful bows that she and Da offered. Mairead remembered one in particular—a lean dark-haired man with silver eyes, walking arm-in-arm with a laughing girl who looked exactly like him.

"Midir and Brigid," Da had whispered. "Son and daughter to the Dagda, the King of the Tuatha dé Danann."

Brigid had paused before Mairead and whispered a few words. When Mairead looked up, a constellation of tiny, transparent orbs floated around her. The orbs caught beams of sunlight, shattered them into rainbows, and then popped with a soft tinkle of music when Mairead touched them with a fingertip.

Mairead had looked up into the smiling faces of the Fae prince and princess. Their joy had suffused her own heart and carried her through her chores for weeks afterward.

But when Da died, Mairead's love for the Tuatha dé Danann turned sour. She knew that only a few of them possessed healing powers; she understood that they could not heal everyone. But she hated that they were so invulnerable, rarely affected by sickness at all. She hated that their lives stretched into century after century, when Da had but fifty-two years. He was the best soul she had ever known, and he died, while the Tuatha dé Danann glided through time untouched.

A sour piece of her soul had rejoiced when she saw they could burn and die like any other.

But now, crushed and bowed over in the center of the road, barely able to stay on her feet, Mairead realized what they had done for the land and its people—what they had provided, and the evil they had held back.

She dared not pray to them. They were gone. It was a wrong she had not done herself, but she had not tried to stop it, either. If she had tried to interfere, she might have burned with them.

But perhaps then her soul would have been clean.

She could not pray to the dead, but perhaps an older divinity would accept her petition.

"Danu, Goddess Intangible," she whispered. "Forgive me. And help me, though I do not deserve it."

Her fingers pierced the hard crust of the loaf she held, delving into the soft center.

She waited. Expecting a sign, or some influx of strength.

And also expecting nothing at all. Because why should Danu care? Why should anyone care if one lonely Mairead burst into bloody fragments, her soul drifting away on the wind?

I care.

The voice was quiet, inveterate, bitter and sweet, like the taste of blood or metal.

She cared. Mairead cared to exist. Beyond hope, beyond reason, beyond any certainty of a better future—she would exist because doing so was her power. Survival in this dread world was a glory in itself.

Her foot lifted, heavy as stone. Shifted forward, and planted itself again.

One step. And another. And she was walking.

A spasm of raw hunger wrenched through her gut, and she chewed desperately at the bread while she walked.

The loaf was long gone when she staggered through the tangle of the forest into the clearing where Cashel's hut stood. His hovel was an untidy jumble of boards and logs and stones, heaped over with packed dirt and coated with moss. It resembled a beaver's lodge more than a house.

Mairead's stomach gurgled and surged, and she choked with horror, pressing her fingers to her mouth. She wanted nothing more than to vomit, to heave the creature from her body. But if what Saoirse said was true, that would only hasten her end.

Her muscles were weak and liquid now, deprived of sustenance as the *alp-luachra* consumed everything. With hands that trembled like frail autumn leaves, Mairead reached for the door of the hut—she could not even knock, she could only scrape at the wood as she slid down, crumpling to the earth. She tilted her head against the door and closed her eyes.

The door popped open, and Mairead tumbled across the threshold. She blinked up into the broad face of Cashel O'Carney.

Cashel was known for several things, but the foremost was his long dark hair, which reached well past his waist and remained perpetually glossy and smooth. Several strands of it drifted across Mairead's cheeks as he leaned over her.

"Well met, Mairead," he said gruffly. "If you're unwell, you'd best see Saoirse. I've naught of herbs and potions here."

"We both know that's not true," she murmured. "Saoirse obtains ingredients from you. River weed, and water plants.

"That's between me and the midwife." Cashel rubbed his jaw with a massive hand. "I was sorry to hear about your Da. He was a good man."

Mairead closed her eyes again. "Aye. He was."

"May I help you up? You look as if you could use a drink, lass."

"Lass." She snorted, but accepted his outstretched hand. "I'm no lass, O'Carney. I'm a woman grown."

"So I see. But I'm eight years your elder, and I remember you coming here with your Da when you were a wee slip of a thing. You'll always be that lass to me. Come and sit down."

Mairead collapsed into one of two rough-hewn chairs in the hovel, breathing in the scent of onions and fish, salt and pine. A strong combination, but not unpleasant. The aroma cleared her mind.

"I don't have much time." She laid a hand on her expanding belly. "I need your help."

Cashel's brown eyes widened. "Ah, I see. You're needing a protector, someone to give your wee spawn a name. It's a big thing to ask of me, Mairead. Sure, and I was a friend of your father's, but I don't know about taking on his daughter and her babe—"

"I'm not asking you to marry me!" she snapped. "I need as much salted fish as you can give me. No questions."

"Salted fish?"

"Yes. You have stores of it?"

"I do, but—"

"I'll take it all. You can have a piece of my land in exchange."

Cashel frowned. "A piece of your land? What would I do with a piece of your land? I'll not give up my winter's supply for a bit of cracked dirt."

Mairead's stomach twisted, the warning of an oncoming bout of hunger. "You can have all the land, as long as I get to stay in the cottage."

"No." Cashel folded his arms. "I'm no farmer. I get by with what I glean from the woods and rivers. I've no need of plows and furrows and fences."

"Please, Cashel. I need the fish. All of it, or as much as it takes—"

"And what are you planning to do with it? Eat it all yourself? Sell it?"

"I can't tell you. Please. Is there anything I can offer—the house, with all that's in it—it's not much, but perhaps—" An idea gripped Mairead's mind, terrible and compelling. "You can—you can take me, as payment. For the fish."

"Take you? Haven't I said I don't want to be saddled with a wife and babe?"

"No." She rose unsteadily, gripping the back of the chair for support. Cashel was not a tall man, and she could look him in the eye. "You don't have to marry me. You can—have me. After it's done—I mean, I'll return later today. Tonight."

Cashel stared, his mouth slightly open.

"I know I'm not much to look at. God knows I've worked myself to the bone. But I'm not hideous, am I?" Mairead's hands writhed into her skirts, clutching them convulsively.

"Far from it," said Cashel gently. "What happened to you, lass? Why are you so desperate for food? You can share my noon meal, if you like, but I'll not take your body as payment."

Mairead ground her lip between her teeth until the blood came. Her stomach was cramping again, spasming and twisting. A groan leaked from her throat in spite of her efforts to hold it back.

"Mairead?" Cashel caught her arm as she pitched forward.

"Saoirse told me not to tell anyone," she whispered. "But I am going to die anyway, so I might as well confess. I have an *alp-luachra* in my belly. It crawled into my mouth while I slept in the field, and it is growing. I have one chance to get it out, and that is to drive it mad with thirst. I need all the salt fish you can spare, to feed it, so it will leave me and make for the river."

Cashel's face turned stark white under the sleek mane of his hair. He swallowed, his gaze darted down to Mairead's shifting belly. "Danu preserve us," he breathed.

"So now you see." Tears slid from Mairead's eyes.

He nodded. "I'll get the fish. And you'll need someone on hand to kill the creature when it comes out."

Moments later they trudged toward the river together. Mairead chewed and swallowed salt fish as fast as she could, while Cashel carried a bag of fish in one hand and an axe in the other.

The fish tasted delicious at first. Mairead had not eaten such plump, well-preserved, flavorful fish in years. "Where do you catch these?"

Cashel shrugged. "You have to know where to look."

"But I saw no fishing tackle, no rods or nets, in your home. How do you snare them?"

He stared ahead, his eyes fixed on the glittering ribbon of the river, visible through the trees ahead. "That is a conversation for another time."

Upon reaching the river, they found a large rock whose surface sloped down toward the water. On another day, the rock might have been sun-warm, a delightful spot to rest and watch the play of the sparkling water. But today, the sky was dull, strewn with thin gray clouds that dimmed the light but yielded no rain. The river itself was little more than a stream now, sunken low in its bed. Mairead felt similarly low and sluggish, but she forced herself to continue to eat. She took bite after bite of the dried fish, chewing and swallowing, trying not to gag. Her gums felt fuzzy, and the insides of her cheeks had gone dry. Her throat ached for cool water.

Cashel handed her another piece of fish.

"I'm sorry," she managed, despite her thirst-thickened tongue. "It must be hard to watch all your hard work disappearing down my gullet."

"I'll survive," he said. "It's those who buy from me that I'm worried for."

Mairead stopped mid-chew. She hadn't thought of those who came to Cashel for fish. She had thought only of herself, as usual.

"Others may starve because of me." She shoved the piece of fish at him. "You may as well kill me now then, for I won't allow more lives to end while I stand idly by."

"Slow death by starvation, or having your insides ripped open while a monster and its newborns slither out? I'd not call that 'standing idly by,' lass."

Mairead couldn't see his expression through her tears. "Enough people have died, don't you think? It's wrong, all of it. The human deaths happening now, through drought and starvation and disease—they are but the penalty for our sins against the Fae."

Cashel's eyes heated. "Speak like that, and you'll find yourself lashed to a pyre or bundled into one of the druids' wicker men."

"I don't care. I'm dead anyway."

"You're not." He pressed the piece of fish back into her hand. "Eat. It may mean nights of hard, dangerous work, but I'll find a way to replenish my stores of fish, never fear. None will starve if I can help it. But today, the life that matters is yours."

The force of his tone salved Mairead's guilt a little. He sounded so confident, so determined to work as hard as need be. She admired that kind of grit in a man.

She sank her teeth into the skin and flesh of the fish, plucking aside a stray bone. Maybe she could survive this. Maybe she could work with Cashel and help him catch more fish from whatever secret watering hole he knew.

The fish had been tasty at first, but now the heaviness of the salt was cloying. It burned on her lips until the delicate skin cracked, and each chunk seared the inside of her mouth. Slowly, bite by painful bite, she managed to work her way through two more pieces of fish, but by the third, she could hardly think. She could not focus on anything but the ripple of the river, so close. So limpid and refreshing. If she could only dip her fingers into that glistening flow and dribble a few drops of cool water over her salt-scorched tongue.

She collapsed onto her swollen belly, crawling down the rock toward the water.

"Mairead." Cashel rumbled a warning. "Do not drink."

"Just a little," she wheezed.

"No." He seized her shoulders, turning her onto her back. "Lie still here, and wait. And while you wait, have a little more fish."

"No." She twisted her head aside. "I have had enough."

He sighed and turned away for a moment. She thought he had given up, but he pulled a small bag from the pouch at his waist. "Here." And he gripped her jaw, forcing it open, and dribbled pure salt into her mouth.

Mairead screeched as the grains burned on her sensitive tongue and tumbled down her dry throat. She bucked against Cashel's grip, trying to fling herself into the water, but he held on until she quieted.

The creature in her belly did not settle, though. It squirmed and writhed, slithering under and over itself, restless with craving. Mairead looked up, between the long locks of Cashel's hair, into his eyes. "Almost," she whispered. "So close now. Thank you, but you should step aside. I need to do this part alone."

He nodded, scooting back on the rock and curling his fingers around the handle of the axe.

Mairead lay still, drinking the power of the rock beneath her. Steady, immoveable. She would become like the rock—stone everlasting, stoic and strong, and able to do what must be done.

She stretched her jaws apart as far as they would go, and waited. No luscious stream of water an arm's length away could move her. Much as she might yearn to plunge her face and her body into that blessed flow, she would not. She would lie here until thirst drained the dregs of her life and she shriveled into a formless husk; but she would never give in to the *alp-luachra*. She would suffer through the burning in her mouth and the pain in her stomach—the burning and the pain that was her rightful penance, a fraction of what she owed for the burning and pain of the Tuatha dé Danann.

Her belly lurched and swayed. And then a sickening fullness began, starting just below her lungs and oozing upward. She could feel the channel from her stomach to her mouth widening, stretching, straining under the slow progress of the creature.

Perhaps she would burst apart inside, blood and acid flooding the cavity of her chest. Perhaps the creature would linger too long in her throat and she would suffocate. The salt of her tears scorched the corners of her eyes as the *alp-luachra* crawled further up, under her ribs.

Mairead sucked in a huge, desperate breath before the body of the monster cut off her air passage. It probed the back of her throat, tickling the entrance to her sinus cavity before sluggishly dragging itself over her tongue and teeth. Mairead couldn't see it, couldn't do anything but exist, and pray for air, and endure the sensation of the massive, sludgy monster oozing from her bowels, under her ribs, and out between her lips. A final heave, and a nauseating splash of bile, and it was gone.

With a cry, Cashel leaped forward, stamping his boot on one end of the creature.

Mairead flipped over and retched. Her stomach, chest, and throat were burning, acid licking like flames where the monster had passed. Cashel's axe descended in a whistling arc, its edge ringing against stone as it bit through the monster. The *alp-luachra's* body burst, spewing half-digested bits of fish across the rock. It was slug-shaped, with jelly-like legs and feelers and a sharp-toothed maw at one end. Where Cashel's boot pressed it, spines sprang out of its bulbous carcass, and when he lifted his foot, the spines retracted. At the creature's center, in a slick bulging sack, the half-formed young were gestating.

Mairead could not speak to ask if the Unseelie monster was dead. But she dragged herself up, blood flecking the saliva that blew from her lips with every harsh breath; and she took the axe from Cashel. She chopped, and chopped, and chopped, until there was nothing left of the *alp-luachra* or its foul spawn, except smears of goo and gore along the rock.

When she was done, Mairead threw aside the axe and plunged into the river. Shallow as it was, it posed no danger, though she was not a great swimmer.

She drank only a mouthful of the water, for the river sometimes carried sickness. She would wait and drink her fill later. For now, it was enough that she was alone in her own body, that she was immersed and clean and free.

Clearing the surface again, she shook the drops from her eyes and moved feebly toward the shore again. As her moment of triumph faded, her body's clamor returned. She was sick with hunger and exhaustion, ravaged inside from the passage of the creature. She would need to eat thin soup, and rest, and heal. But there was no one to make any soup for her, or to care for the farm while she rested.

She clawed her way to a bare patch of rock where there were no *alp-luachra* entrails. Cashel sat nearby, his knees drawn up and his dark hair flowing over his shoulders and body like a cape.

"I did not know you were in such dire straits," he said. "Perhaps I should have known. But I took no time to think on it."

"I am not your responsibility." Mairead's voice was a thin rasp, and Cashel winced.

"Don't speak," he said. "Not now, not until you are better. If you would stay with me, and allow me to care for your health a while, I would be grateful."

Mairead's aching body twitched with apprehension. Would he now claim a reward of her?

"I want nothing from you," he said. "Consider it the balance of a debt I owe your father—one that I should have been more ready to repay when you first asked for my help."

"What debt?" She shaped the words with her lips only, letting her aching throat rest.

"Your father kept my secret," said Cashel. "And if you and I are to be friends, I must trust you with it as well. You asked how I obtain the fattest fish, the best river plants?" He rose to his full height, stripping off his leather pouch, his tunic, his boots, and his trousers. Mairead watched, numb with weariness and shock, barely alert enough to admire the solid shape of his body.

And then his long dark hair swirled around him, sucking to his skin while his form shrank and shifted. His face grew smaller, darker, and whiskery.

She blinked, and where Cashel had been sat a sleek river otter, larger than any she had ever seen, its upper body propped on its webbed front paws. Sharp claws arched from those paws—claws that were perfect for catching fish.

A selkie.

Cashel O'Carney—a selkie.

Mairead's heart swelled with pain and purpose. She wanted to say, *You are safe with me. I will keep your secret as my father did.*

But her throat was too wounded. Her voice and her body would take time to heal. Instead, she reached out and ran her fingertips along the creature's thick pelt—a wordless promise.

The selkie nosed her palm, then slithered down the rock and leaped into the water, flinging up a rainbow of sparkling drops. He swam effortlessly, like rain flowing over leaves.

And Mairead laughed inside, in the echoing emptiness of herself, a hollow space that she could fill with anything and everything now.

The People of Danu were gone. But the Fae were not.

2

THE

TWELFTH
HUNTER

Long ago, the gods were born from the eternal essence of the universe. Beirgid, goddess of lust and fertility, came from the pulsing heart of a red star. Aine, goddess of youth and beauty, burst from the sparkling fragments of a yellow star. Macha, goddess of war, broke out of the ruins of two stars that had collided. And Arawn was born from the darkness between the stars.

The other gods were born of stars, and they did not understand Arawn, who was made of the darkness. When the other gods created a world full of living creatures, Arawn cultivated dark plants with thorns and poisons. He said that danger would make the humans and animals live more carefully, and help them value their existence all the more.

But humans are foolish. And instead of living carefully, or valuing their existence, they became greedy and brutish. One day, twelve men pursued a beautiful stag through the forest, intent on capturing it and taking its horns. At that time, death did not exist, and no human tongue had yet tasted meat. But the men craved the splendid antlers of the stag, and so they dragged it down and began to saw the antlers off. The stag cried out, but the other gods did not like to hear any sound except joy from their creations, and they stopped their ears.

The stag cried again, and Arawn heard his cry. Arawn sent a wall of poisonous, thorny vines to encircle the twelve hunters. Eleven of them abandoned their prey and tried to escape. Each one was poisoned by the thorns and died. The twelfth hunter cut the whole head off the stag and used the antlers to shove his way through the vines to safety.

The souls of the eleven hunters slipped from their bodies and circled the thicket of thorns, wailing. When the other gods saw what had happened, they blamed Arawn for causing the first eleven human deaths. They told him he must make a place for the souls to go, where no one could hear their noise. And so he made the land of Unlife, Annwn. Entrances to his world appear as pits lined with writhing black vines, and they appear only in the deepest, oldest forests. The dead pass through these pits into Arawn's world, where they are judged in his furnace of souls and then sent to their eternal resting place in Annwn.

The twelfth hunter, who had cut off the stag's head, went back to the thicket with an ax and chopped away the vines. He dragged the stag's carcass to his village and began to burn it—but then he discovered that it smelled delicious, and he tasted some of the meat. He shared the venison with other humans, and they began to look at other creatures, not as their companions, but as prey.

But Arawn would not let the twelfth hunter's crimes go unpunished. He transformed the souls of the other eleven hunters into fierce death-hounds with eyes of fire, and together they chased down the one who had taken the stag's head. While his hounds chewed the last hunter to bits, Arawn himself took the head of the stag and fashioned it into a mask—the mask of the Horned King. By doing so he honored the stag, and he became a symbol of fear and death to all humans who would commit violence.

3

THE

PIED

PIPER

It started quite simply—small jobs here and there. An infestation of termites at a roadside inn. A flock of crows decimating local crops. Clouds of locusts chewing into the hay and promising a bone-thin winter for the waggoners' horses.

I designed a different song for each type of creature—wove their primal desires into an irresistible medley, teased and tempted them until they were caught helpless in the net of the notes. And then—then I twisted the net tight, and they pranced merrily to their doom, whether it be fire, flood, or fall, whichever happened to be handy. With the crows it was tricky—I led them into a lightning storm, and nearly fried myself while ensuring their destruction.

But in the end I walked away, twirling the pipe, while the field behind me bristled black with stiff, motionless wings.

The farmers made pies of the birds, or so I heard. A frugal use indeed.

One cursed evening, after hours of trudging the dusty roads, I entered a tavern and ordered a bowl of soup. It was watery, dotted with chunks of fibrous vegetable. I gnawed one such lump slowly, grinding it to pulp between my teeth and pondering my next destination. I was beginning to ache for the delicate fare of home.

Each Faerie from my clan had to spend their hundredth year in the human world, using no magic except what was contained within a single object. My parents were occupied with Faerie politics, so it fell to my elder sister to assign my magical item. When she handed me the pipe, crafted by pixies and imbued with a milder form of their compulsive dance magic, my heart swelled tight. It was the most beautiful thing I had ever seen— cinnamon-colored wood matching my own mop of curls, with shining brass fixtures along its length.

"I know you love music," my sister had said. "I thought perhaps it would comfort you, and provide for you during your stay among the humans. I have heard that many of them delight in music. Perhaps they would be willing to pay for your skill."

It was a gracious thought. But it had been two hundred years since her sojourn, so perhaps she had forgotten how churlish humans could be. I had soon discovered that they would drink my music eagerly with their ears, but turn their backs the moment I asked for a spare coin in exchange for the song. They were so greedy in their consumption, so miserly in their appreciation—it soured my heart.

I had been out of work for three weeks when I entered that tavern, gnawed that tough bit of vegetable, and heard of Hamelin for the first time. I was nearly at the end of my sojourn year, weary and worn from scraping by on the meager generosity of humans. Hunched in my cape at a corner table, I sipped broth and listened to a group of merchants swapping tales of the towns they'd passed through.

"I'll not go back to Hamelin," growled one of them. "Spent one night there. Sold a few coins' worth of wares, and when I woke the next morning, the rats had got into my clay pots and jars. Some of the bowls were chewed clean through. Every dish, every mug had at least one rat dropping, and some even had broods of squirming young. I had to take the lot to the river and wash it all. Even then you could still smell the rat droppings. The goodwives in the next town took one sniff of my wares and turned up their noses. Months of work, wasted."

"I traveled through there a while back," said another man. "I thought there'd be plenty of work for a carpenter, what with all them rats, and there was. But every time I nailed a board, the rats chewed through somewhere else. The townspeople wouldn't pay me. Stingy lot. Lazy, too. Did you see how they make the little ones do the work?"

The potter nodded. When he leaned forward, every man at the table shifted toward him instinctively, hungry for the secrets he was about to divulge. "The children are raised like slaves. Even the tiny ones who can barely walk are taught to wash and cook and clean, while the grown men and women eat, drink, and lie about. It's shameful, that's what it is." He gave an emphatic nod and poured a generous swallow of ale down his throat. "Stay clear of Hamelin, that's what I say."

Shifting back my hood a little, I raised my voice. "Excuse me, sirs. Which direction is Hamelin?"

All the men twisted toward me, their faces every shade from annoyed to hostile. The potter looked me up and down, swiping his mouth with his sleeve. "What's that now?"

"Which way is Hamelin, if you would be so kind?"

"Listening in on a private conversation, were ya?"

"My apologies." I forced a smile. "It is a small tavern, and your voices are so wonderfully strong."

The potter snorted and returned to his drink, but the carpenter said, "If you heard our talk, you heard what we said about Hamelin. A lazy, miserly, backwards town. Not the sort of place you'd want to go, lad."

"Oh, I don't know about that," said a burly man. "This one looks odd enough to fit right in among them Hamelin tossers. What sort of cloak is that now, boy-o? Your mum stitch it together from the scraps o' your wee nappies?"

He roared with laughter, and the others joined in.

I touched the colorful patchwork of my cape. It was no use explaining that this cape, along with my mismatched clothes, would protect me from being discerned and targeted by Unseelie Fae. Without this pied outfit of mine, I would likely have been assimilated by a Soul-Eater or crunched up in the jaws of some were-beast or other.

No use explaining that to these louts, however. Humans were growing less and less aware of magic as the centuries passed by. They would likely laugh all the harder if I attempted an explanation.

Contrary to human superstition, the Fae can lie. I drew my pipe from beneath my cape and said softly, "My father was a rag-and-bone man. Left my mother and me destitute. When I tracked him down, I made these clothes for myself using his wares. What was lacking in material I made up for with pieces of his skin. And this pipe?" I lifted it up, and their eyes followed the movement. "I whittled the keys from the joints of his spine."

They stared at me, clearly unsure whether laughter or terror might be the correct response.

My lips pulled back in a wicked smile, and the potter swore. "You're a sick braggart, you are. You take us for fools?"

"I would never take you anywhere," I said. "You're not my type at all."

The man's cheeks reddened. "What's that now?"

The burly man slammed down his mug and rose from his seat, cracking his knuckles.

"Come 'ere, you. I'll teach you how to talk to yer betters."

As he circled the table, I set my pipe to my lips and began to play.

Usually I plied my magic only on animals and insects. When I played for humans, I followed their own familiar folk tunes, restraining the magic of the pipe, resisting its temptation to wander off into the wilds of Fae music. Though not strictly forbidden, the magical control of human minds was frowned upon by my clan.

But I had used Fae music on humans twice before, during my year in this world. The first time was in an orphanage where the matron gave me shelter in exchange for a song for the children. Their sad, hollow eyes mirrored an ache within me, so I played with fresh fervor until their faces brightened and they began to dance around the shabby common room. I played to them until bedtime, when I switched to a lullaby and ushered them gently into dreamland.

The second time, I had come upon a ragged troupe of performers who were trying vainly to interest a village crowd on market day. The troupe was talented, and I felt the same sympathetic stirring within myself—a passion to help them succeed. When I played that time, the entire market crowd danced in the street for hours. Afterward they frowned and trotted off home with many complaints of sore feet, but they did not share their coin with me or the performers. No matter, for a clever boy in the troupe had scrabbled about on the cobbles while the people were dancing, gathering up any stray coins that happened to shake out of their pockets and purses. It was a good day for the troupe, and once we were well away from the town, they gave me a portion of the earnings.

On this night, as the burly, red-faced man stormed toward me, I fed my anger and bitterness into the pipe, and out spiraled a song fierce and furious, one that spun him around where he stood and marched him to the center of the room.

Dance, you fool, dance. The words echoed in my mind and bled through the music. *Dance until you bleed.*

And he did. They all did, every man and woman in the tavern, from the innkeeper and his wife, to the cook and the serving girl. I made them dance until their feet swelled and their shoes broke and their blisters burst. Every bit of rage in my heart slithered from my soul, through the pipe, into their ears, until my fingers were bruised from playing.

When it was done, I stalked through the common room, stepping over weeping bodies, and I swept out into the darkness.

I walked all night, stopping at a farmhouse just before dawn to glean directions to Hamelin. The town glowed like an ember in my mind—the grand culmination of all I had borne and done this year. When I saw the smoke of its fires on the horizon, my heart pulsed fiercely, and I had to pause on the lip of a ridge to take in the view.

Hamelin was a collection of crooked houses, second and third stories propped on stilts or supported by the shoulders of adjacent buildings. Beyond a strip of scraggly farms flowed a dark river, shaded by heavy-limbed trees. The forest circled the valley like the arms of a monster, drawing tighter and tighter in an embrace of murderous passion. Nature wanted the valley back—wanted to swallow it again and reduce it to fertile fodder for thick roots.

A sour wind rushed up to me, fluttering through my garments, and I lifted my head to its reek, undeterred. Gleeful, even. I could sense my doom or destiny in this place.

As I strode down the hill and through the fields, I noticed the wilting stalks of grain, nibbled by numberless tiny teeth. The few people I saw tending to the crops were not men at all, but boys, none of them above age fifteen, and several younger than twelve. A few of them had clustered around a girl, maybe seven years old, who hunched under the weight of a yoke and two wooden buckets. The laborers passed around a dipper, partaking of the water within.

I approached them, but they shrank from me and scattered back into the fields. The little girl with the yoke struggled to hurry away.

"Please," I called to her. "I am thirsty. I swear I will not harm you."

She hesitated and turned back, her blue eyes round in her smudged face.

Closer I came, palms out. "I carry no weapon, and I mean you no ill. Only spare me a drink if you would be so kind."

She nodded, tangled curls bobbing from beneath her brown headscarf.

Reaching out, I lifted the yoke. She rubbed her shoulders as I eased the buckets to the ground. "There. Is that better? Why do you carry such a heavy load?"

She only stared, so I drank deeply and then hoisted the yoke onto my own shoulders. "I will carry it to the village for you."

Vehemently she shook her head.

"And why not?" I asked.

"It is my task," she whispered. "Sharing the work is not permitted."

"What if I carry it a little way, and then return it to you before we reach the gate?"

She pinched her lips, pondering, then gave me a quick nod. We walked toward the town, while the child stole glances at me. "Are you a beggar?" she asked.

"Not exactly. People pay me to chase away pests. Crows, locusts, mice—"

"Rats?" Her eyes lit up.

"Yes. I hear you have some trouble with them."

"They eat all the food we can gather. They chew through cupboards and boxes. Some of them are big, like this." She held up her arms, shaping something about the size of a barn cat.

"I have never seen rats so large."

"They are," she affirmed. "We cannot leave the babies alone, or they will be eaten. The rats like the soft parts, eyes and tongue and fingers. Conrad's parents were out drinking the other night, and he was finishing some work in the stables while little Cristina slept. When he heard screams he ran back inside and there were two big ones in her bed. They chewed two of her fingers to the bone."

Horror bit deep into my soul. "You say their parents were out?"

"While we are young, we work." Her blue eyes held an ache too raw for one so young. "When we are grown, we may eat and drink and play games, as our parents do. They worked when they were children, and now they deserve their leisure. They gave us life. They are worthy of our service."

"Are they indeed," I said dryly. "And how many years until you join the happy ranks of the adults?"

"When I am sixteen," she said. "I am ten now."

"Ten?" She was so small and thin. I had thought her years younger. "And how many brothers and sisters do you have?"

"Eight. My parents needed many of us to work hard, so they could enjoy their best years."

"It is not so in other places," I told her. "In most villages, the adults work, and the children help a little, but they also play and do lessons. Have you a school in Hamelin?"

"What is a school?"

"A place where someone teaches you how to do sums, how to read and write."

The child lowered her voice. "Dorothea teaches numbers and letters to some of the older ones at night. They must gather two or three at once, in secret. But the rats chewed up the two books she had. She cried so many tears, I thought her eyes might melt away."

"Who is in charge of your village?"

"Burgomeister Rottmundin. He leads the council."

"I shall have a word with him about this plague of rats." Even as I spoke the words, several rats scuttled boldly across the path, from one field to another. They were ash-gray creatures with bulky haunches, sharp noses, and eyes as stony black as any Unseelie monster I had ever seen. Their tails writhed wormlike behind them.

"Give me my yoke," said the child urgently. "We are nearing the gates."

I returned the burden to her. "Thank you for your kindness, and for your conversation." I took a crust from my satchel—the only morsel of food I had left—and handed it to her.

Her eyes widened. "For me?"

"Of course."

She staggered away, one hand bracing the yoke while the other crammed the bread into her mouth. Clenching my teeth, I turned away from the sight of her—the slanted bones of her thin shoulders, and her tattered tunic flapping around her twig-thin legs.

But as I entered the town, traversing streets that stank of offal and rot, I could not ignore the ragged urchins shoring up unsteady buildings and hammering horseshoes. One girl was dipping candles, her fingers scarred shiny from years of contact with hot wax. A boy was butchering rats and roasting them over a metal grill; the foul fat sizzled as it dripped into the flames. Tots who had barely learned to walk were scrubbing clothes in washtubs.

I had seen my share of poor children during my sojourn, but the young of Hamelin were neglected in a manner worse than poverty. Their enslavement was a cruel reversal of life's natural order. It seemed I had stumbled upon a dark pit in the world, where parental love was entirely absent. I half-hoped there was dread magic at work; but I could feel no lingering echo of it in the air. No reason for the cruelty, except the convergence and mutual degeneration of a hundred avaricious souls.

A few adults strolled the streets, dressed in bright clothes speckled with holes from rat teeth. Some of the men and women carried canes topped with colorful ribbons, and they used the pointed tips to prod any child who seemed to be slacking or slowing at his task.

I approached a trio of the townspeople, trying to smile despite the sickening of my heart. "Good sir, I am looking for Burgomeister Rottmundin."

The man paused, and so did the two ladies clutching his arms. All of them looked well-fed, and had the soft, neat hands of idle nobility.

But under their layers of cheap, cloying perfume, they smelled strongly of rat excrement—and I could swear I saw a tail dangling from one woman's handbag, though it whisked inside the next second.

"We don't care for strangers here," the man said. "Unless they have wares to sell, or they've come to buy ours."

"I have no wares."

"My daughters make lace and ribbons," interjected one of the women. "We would be happy to sell you some."

"My children make fine dinnerware and lovely trinkets out of tin," said the other woman. "Much more durable than *her* rat-nibbled ribbons."

"Your pardon, but I am not looking to purchase wares, either," I said.

"Then you'd best take yourself off," growled the man.

"If you would direct me to Burgomeister Rottmundin—"

"I said, you have no business here."

"No business? I thought you had trouble with rats."

"Every town has trouble with rats," he grumbled, but one of the women leaned forward eagerly. "We have the most terrible plague of rats. Swarms of them, some as tiny as a child's fist and some larger than a fox."

"It's the children's fault," the second woman added. "They do not clean the houses well, or store the food properly, or dispose of the filth quickly enough. It's a disgrace. *Some people* are not strict enough with the training and correction of their offspring." She cast a disparaging glance at her rival before looking back at me. "What are you, a rat-catcher?"

"Something far more effective." I smiled grimly at her.

"The Burgomeister's house is down the next street," the man grunted. "There is an emblem of a crowned owl above the door."

"My thanks to you." I did not give them the courtesy of either a nod or a bow, but moved on quickly, eager to be done with this job and this place. I could have gone on my way and forgotten all about the misery I'd witnessed; but I could not depart without alleviating a little of the children's suffering, and if I could do so by eliminating the rats, then I must.

The Burgomeister's youngest daughter greeted me—a child of four, who asked haltingly if she could take my satchel and cloak. When I declined, she ushered me into her father's study. The room reeked of ale and an unfamiliar tobacco blend. The Burgomeister lay upon a couch, his eyes half-lidded and his body draped with velvet and lace, while one of his sons massaged his puffy feet with liniment. The cushions of the divan on which he sprawled had been chewed in several places, and as he greeted me I saw the heads of baby rats poking out of a hole in the pillow under his elbow. Another rat was struggling to clamber out of the tankard of ale on the floor by the divan.

The Burgomeister's eyes glittered at me between the swollen pouches of his lids. "What do you want?"

"I see that you do not stand on ceremony," I replied. "It is just as well—I am in no mood for pleasantries. I am here to rid your town of all its rats."

He laughed, a deep rolling bellow. "All the rats? Gone? Like that?" He snapped his fingers. "You must be joking."

"I swear to you, I am not. Pay me well, and I will purge this place of every last rat."

His eyes narrowed to slits. "Every last rat, eh?"

"I will destroy them all. For a price."

"Of course, for a price. No one does anything without payment. Except children, of course." He nodded to the boy massaging his gouty feet. "But they don't know any better, do they? And they're still working off the life-debt they owe us for their existence. Tell me, what do you think of our ways?"

It was a trap, of course. If I insulted him, he would offer me less money. Flatter him, and perhaps he would pay more.

I was nearly at the end of my sojourn, and I had nothing. I was entirely beggared, worn thin, with pockets as empty as my heart. My cousin had returned from her sojourn with a chest of jewels from human admirers. My elder brother had brought home fine weapons crafted by the best of human artisans. And I, the worthless wanderer with my winsome melodies—what did I have to show for my months in human company? Nothing but a growing distaste for human beings in general, and the Burgomeister in particular.

Facing my family with empty hands and a forlorn heart was a shame I did not think I could bear. This was my final chance to bring back something, if only a little silver.

"I admire your innovation, my lord," I told the man, with a sweeping bow. "You have designed a way of life that is truly unique."

"And yet so few appreciate its beautiful simplicity." He picked up the tankard, seized the drowning rat by its scruff, and flung it against the wall so hard that it splattered red goo and fell broken to the floor. "Clean that up," he told his son.

As the boy hurried to obey, the Burgomeister rose from the couch and hoisted a small chest onto the heavy writing table. From the chest he removed three small bags. "There are a thousand guilders here. I'll give you fifty now, and the rest when you accomplish your task. Every last rat gone from the town."

"Very well." I stretched out my hand, and he gripped it in his.

Then he yanked me nearer, his hot breath foul on my face.

"There's something strange about you, boy," he said. "Take off that hood, and let's have a look at you."

My curly hair was usually thick and voluminous enough to hide my pointed ears, but the hood served as an extra measure against discovery. "Removing my hood wasn't part of the deal," I said evenly.

"Where are you from, then?"

"Around, and sometimes Above, but never Below."

The Burgomeister's brows scrunched together, as if he was trying to puzzle out my riddle. Finally he gave up and said, "You have called my bluff, lad—I don't care who you are or where you're from, as long as you do the work. The deal is struck. Off with you, and do what you can. I'll give you three days." And he grinned, showing stained and broken teeth. Perhaps he thought the deadline would be impossible for me to meet.

"Three days?" I grinned back. "I'll only need one."

The Burgomeister snorted. He counted out the fifty guilders, which I tucked into my satchel. Then he scrawled on a scrap of paper and handed it to me. "You can stay at the inn down the street. Give them this note, and they'll grant you lodging for free. They've got extra guests, those whose homes have been overrun with swarms of rats, but they'll have a cot to spare."

Darkness draped the corners and alleyways as I walked the streets of Hamelin, my ragged garments billowing in the breeze. Despite their duties, the children were only children, and they shrank from me, frightened of the stranger stalking through their midst. I must have looked rather fell, with my height and my hood, and the Fae pipe clutched in my hand. I had thought of driving out the rats that very evening, but I was weary to the bone. I'd had little rest the previous night, and I'd been traveling all day. To fuel its power, the pipe drained some energy from me with every use, and I was reluctant to use it until I'd had dinner and a full night's sleep.

The inn was flanked by a tavern on one side and what appeared to be a brothel on the other. Perhaps not strictly a brothel, but certainly a place where the citizens of Hamelin came to do deeds of ill repute. A young man in dazzling purple, with chewed-up ribbons at his throat, reached for me as I passed. "Show us your face, love. I'll warrant it's a pretty one."

"Excuse me," I muttered, heading for the door of the inn.

"What's wrong, precious? You shy?" squawked a female voice behind me, and thin fingers yanked back my hood. "Ah, there you are!"

"That's not a face to hide, love," said the young man in purple, sidling closer. "Join us for a drink, won't you?"

"I'm busy." I jerked my hood back into place. "Keep your fingers off, or lose them."

"A spicy one! Oh, I do like 'em spicy!" The women ignored my warning, walking her fingers up my shoulder.

I knocked her hand away and forged ahead into the inn. The pair of them remained outside.

The common room looked normal enough, with its cloud of acrid pipe smoke and a film of cooking grease clinging to the chairs. But when I looked closer, my stomach knotted. The drinks and food were being served by mere children, most of them around twelve if I had to guess—though malnutrition made such guesses unreliable.

A woman clad in leather held sway over the room from a fur-draped chair near the fire. One leg was hitched over the chair arm, its black boot kicking jauntily despite a gaping hole near the ankle. The woman was twisting a lock of her dark hair round and round. Something about her posture reeked of ownership, so I moved in her direction. Three young boys with savage expressions moved to block my access, but the woman waved them aside. "Let him through."

"I have come from the mayor." I extended the paper the mayor had given me. "He has hired me to purge your town of the rats, and he requests that you grant me lodging for the night."

The woman's lips twisted. "You hear that, lads and ladies? This scrawny pied scarecrow has come to save us all!"

Uproarious laughter rattled the room. The woman stared at me, smirking, until the merriment faded. Then she crooked her finger at a shadow in the corner. "Dorothea. Show our guest his room."

The shadow moved forward a little. "But, madam—"

"The room, Dorothea," snarled the woman. "The only one left." She reached beside her chair and took up a knotted staff. "Do I need to speak again?"

"No, madam. Come sir, I will show you the room."

I followed the shadowy girl through the kitchen, where children with huge haunted eyes stirred the stew and kneaded the bread. Little ones with sticks stood nearby, smacking rats' heads when they poked out of the holes in the walls.

Something dropped onto the top of my hood and sank sharp little nails through the fabric. I knocked it off, and the rat squirmed on its back before flipping over and scuttling away. A boy who was chopping carrots pinned the fleeing rat's tail with a practiced foot, flipped his carving knife into the air, and sent it hurtling through the rat's neck. I stared at the little splotch of blood, and the severed rodent's head.

Dorothea tugged my sleeve. "The room, sir."

This girl must be the one who taught the others their letters, the one who had lost her books. She wore an over-large brown dress and a long strip of cloth wound around her head. From my vantage point at her back, I could discern nothing else about her. Her size was childlike, but something about the way she moved hinted at maturity. The fingers that curled around the handle of the lantern were slender and tapered, with elegantly arched knuckles.

I squeezed after her up a crooked flight of steps, trying not to retch as my boots crunched over more rat bodies. In all my wanderings, I had never encountered so foul a place, or so massive an infestation.

It was all too obvious that the room I was being given was not a place of honor. Dorothea led me along a narrow corridor with cells barely large enough to accommodate an adult man lying prone. Most of the rooms had no doors, and ragged children gaped at us as we passed. They huddled together on cots or pallets, some asleep, but always one awake, in every cell.

"One always keeps watch." Dorothea's voice drifted back to me. "To keep away the rats and the ravagers."

She glanced backward as she spoke, and in a stray beam of the lantern I saw her face for the first time—golden-brown skin and eyes like liquid night. There was a delicate savagery to her features, a feral prettiness. And she was no child, though I still could not tell her age.

Dorothea pushed open a door at the end of the hall. "Your room for the night." She pressed against the wall as I ducked through the doorway. There was barely enough space for me to stand between the cot and the wall. On wooden pegs hung a spare corset and underthings, and a few scraps of half-chewed paper were piled on the shelf above them.

"This is your room, isn't it?" I looked her in the eyes, and she lifted her chin proudly. "You do not need to give me your room."

"Everywhere else is full," she said. "And the cellar and attic are flooded with rats."

"But where will you sleep?"

"In the hall, or by the hearth. Take your last looks, sir, for this face will likely be eaten away by morning."

"That is unacceptable," I said. "*I* will take the hearth, or the hall."

"I do not know how you plan to destroy the rats, but I'll warrant you need sleep to do it, and you won't get that if they're crawling over you and nibbling on your soft bits all night." She glanced pointedly at my trousers.

"Well, then—I suppose there is nothing else for it." I pushed back my hood. "We will have to share the bed."

I had grown used to the effect my features had on humans. I was by no means the most exquisite of my kind, but I had enough beauty to attract attention. Despite her sharp words and wariness, the girl was not immune to my looks. Her lips parted for an instant, and her eyes flared wider.

The next second she shuttered the expression. "Me, share a bed with a complete stranger? Do you think me an idiot?"

"I swear I will not touch you."

"That will be impossible, as the bed is narrow." She crossed her arms.

"Then I swear I will not harm you."

"And your word should have weight with me, why?"

"Because—" I ran my fingers through my hair, trying to invent a reason why she should trust me. I could find none, except the obvious. "Because if you do not believe me, one of us will be prey for the rats tonight."

The girl's stare cut through me, as if she were flaying open my chest and extracting my heart. She could chew it up and spit it out and I would count it a blessing.

The unbidden thought startled me, as did the quickening of my pulse. I had been thus far immune to the charms of humans, male or female, but this one— "How old are you?" I asked, almost desperately.

"How old do you want me to be?"

"I want the truth," I said, "or I shall make my bed here, in this hall, and you will be the one to suffer my screams while I'm being eaten."

"I've endured plenty of screams," she replied. "Yours will not bother me."

Glaring, I took off my cloak and satchel and threw them to the floor, dropping my pipe on top of the pile. "As you wish." I stretched out to my full length, spanning a few doorways in the process. A couple of children poked their heads out of their cells to peer at me.

"You cannot let him sleep there, Dorothea," chirped a tiny girl. "He will be chewed."

"Hush! Back to your beds," hissed Dorothea. She kicked my shoulder. "Get up, fool."

"Not until you tell me your true age. And if you lie, I will know."

She crouched, leaning down to whisper. "I have told everyone that I am fifteen. In truth I am nearly twenty."

Our ages were comparable, then. At one hundred years, I was considered newly full-grown among the Fae. The age of twenty possessed a similar significance for many human cultures.

I tried to swallow my delight at her answer. "I knew you were older than the others."

"You hoped." Her mouth curved in a half-smile.

I answered with a broad smile of my own, one that had not touched my face since I entered the human world. "Yes."

Collecting my belongings, I leaped up again, conscious of my height compared to hers. She was as short and slight as a pixie, but her ears had the tender roundness of humanity.

"I have duties, but I will return when I can, with food," she said.

"Very well." I stood aside to let her pass.

Dorothea did not come back for more than an hour. I took off my cloak and seated myself cross-legged in the hallway, playing a lullaby for the little ones in the adjacent rooms. A hush drifted over the place, and I wondered if the rats themselves were sleeping.

At last Dorothea crept up and sat near me, removing her scarf to reveal thick, curly hair, black as night. Between the musical phrases she murmured, "The children do not usually settle so quickly."

I shrugged, continuing to play. After a moment she tapped the pipe with one finger. "This is how you do it, then? Is it magic?"

"There is magic within it, yes."

"And magic within you, I'll wager. Don't bother denying it—I saw your ears earlier, when you did this." She ran her fingers through her hair.

I swore softly.

"I will keep your secret if you will keep mine." She touched her chest. "I bind myself flat to appear younger, so I am not taken for marriage. That way I can stay with the little ones, and look out for them."

"How did you come to be here?"

"My parents had a farm in the hills. Bandits attacked and killed them, but I managed to run away. I wandered, half-starved, until I came here. By the time I was strong enough to leave, my heart was already entwined with the children of this town."

She passed me a bowl—sludgy oat porridge with chunks of sausage. I ate the oily mass gratefully while Dorothea retreated to her room. When I joined her, she was already in the bed, clad in a simple tunic and pressed as close to the wall as she could get.

"Close the door," she said. "So the rats cannot enter that way."

I pushed it shut, then lay down with my back to her and tried to ignore the parts of her that were touching me, and the puffs of her breath on the back of my neck.

"I don't sleep well," she whispered. "They frighten me."

"The rats?"

"The rats—and the men."

"But you don't fear me."

"No."

Another moment passed, and then she said, "If we sleep face to face, the rats are less likely to chew on our noses."

My heart pulsed large at the words. Slowly I turned to face her, our breath mingling in the dark. I am not sure which of us moved first—how the corridor of jagged space between our faces closed—but it did, and the charm of her soft lips on mine was better than any music my pipe could yield.

Skittering and gnawing noises issued from the walls during our exchange of quiet kisses. But those sounds faded as her hot tongue laced with mine, as I moved my body closer to hers. Heat roared over my skin—a heat I had not felt in a long time. I could feel the blood rushing to my groin, arousal tightening my trousers.

Dorothea must have felt the hardness pressed to her inner thigh through the fabric. She stilled for a moment, her lips barely touching mine. I drank her soft breaths into myself, and I quivered with a craving more desperate than any I'd experienced for females of my kind.

I longed to tell her what I felt, to ask what sort of magic this was between us, but I feared that speaking might shatter the charm, and it was too beautiful, too precious and unexpected in that wretched place. I did not want to lose it.

And then her fingers—those slender, elegant fingers—probed for the fastenings of my trousers, releasing them.

Softly she nipped at my mouth, and I sank my hand into her abundant hair. I traced the curve of her adorable round ear, and then I inhaled, sharp and short, because her fingers had closed around my length, and she was coaxing it out.

I didn't speak, nor did she—not even when she drew up the hem of her tunic and shifted her body to grant me access. I was Fae, and not in heat—no danger of children—so when she yearned against me, wordlessly questing, I eased myself into her.

We kissed as we coupled—a silent, urgent, writhing act, one I could scarcely believe was happening. I did not question her motives or mine. I let myself feel every swelling sensation, every ripple of ecstasy. I reached between us and tended to her—clumsily, perhaps, but she had likely been as long without physical delight as I had, and she was exquisitely sensitive. I felt her quiver and spasm around me while her entire delicate frame went rigid with the shock of the pleasure. Her tiny gasps burst in my mouth as I kissed her through the moment—and a few seconds later the tightening heat of my body burst, and a wave of bliss like none I'd ever felt rolled through me.

We parted just as quietly as we'd joined, and rearranged our clothing.

With the passing of the pleasure, the consciousness of our surroundings returned, including the clawing and scraping of the rats. Dorothea shivered, and I wrapped my arm around her until her breathing slowed.

Eventually my own racing thoughts dissolved into sleep as well.

When I woke I felt more rested than I had in days. The air held the expectant chill of night just before daybreak.

Dorothea stirred while I was gathering my things. Her voice glided through the dark. "Are you going to do it now? Drive away the rats?"

"I am going to try. This will be the largest task I have ever attempted."

"I believe you can do it."

"And your belief should have weight with me, why?"

I could hear her smile. "Clever boy, casting my own words back at me. You would not have come here unless you thought you could help. I believe you have a good soul."

Wordless, I shrugged my satchel into place and went downstairs.

The common room was deserted—by humans, at least. With each step I took, the carpet of rats parted for me, but they did not flee into the walls. They were bold indeed. By the light of the dying fire, I saw two of the cat-sized rats the water-carrying child had mentioned—big enough to bite off my entire hand. Terror flickered in my heart.

I eyed those rats, thinking of their nature and needs, their essence, their cravings. When I began to play, it was a dark and dreadful melody, full of teeth and claws—but as I followed the spirit of the music, the tune shifted, turning gooey and golden, like cheese or warm sunlight, like nests of soft feathers and buttery rolls and rashers of savory bacon. Every rat in the common room lifted its head and swayed in place, entranced. From the hallways and rooms above, from the cellar below and the passages between the walls, the rats came with a rattling of rafters and a scraping of claws.

I backed out the door of the inn, never ceasing my tune. I stepped into the dark street, and my music echoed through the crisp air, bouncing off brick and stone, singing between the layers of thatch, winging down chimneys and into alleyways.

Slowly I walked along the street, while my fingers danced over the keys. The chill bit my nose and the tips of my ears, slipping through the patchwork cloak. The sheer number of rats pouring out of the buildings sent a bolt of horror through my stomach; I could scarcely force myself to look at their beady eyes, hunched shoulders, and lashing tails.

The filthy tide surged after me. I dared not stop the music, or the rats would devour me, every bit, from brain to bones. Still playing my pipe, I turned into the next street, and from those homes and shops more rats came forth, gnashing their tiny teeth for the joys that my music promised them. The torrent of their insatiable greed matched that of the townspeople themselves.

By the time the sun was high, my fingers were weary of their dance over the keys. My stomach rumbled with hunger, and my mouth was so parched I could barely maintain the tune. My lungs spasmed, and the muscles of my stomach were sore from tensing to project my breath and my sound as far as possible. But I dared not stop. I was nearly finished with the last street.

I had planned my route through the city the night before, while Dorothea was completing her duties downstairs. My goal was the Weser River, glittering not far beyond the outskirts of the town. Walking backward, eyeing the neverending carpet of rats unrolling after me, I stepped onto the rutted road leading to the river.

And I stumbled over a crust of dried mud.

My ankle twisted painfully beneath me, and the pipe dropped from my lips as I staggered.

For a hideous, suspended instant, I faced the rats, and the silence.

A hissing shriek rippled through the sea of black and gray bodies—a demand for the promised satisfaction. The rats surged forward as one.

I set the pipe to my mouth and resumed the song, trying not to let my fear bleed through as a quickening of the tune or a missed note. Backward I walked, more carefully this time, leading the rats along the road. The pain from my ankle speared through my leg, but I had to keep moving, keep playing. More of the rodents issued from the fields, rivulets of scampering feet joining the great stream of bodies. On I marched, with my dread army, until I stood in the shallows of the rushing river. There had been rain recently, and the central part of the river was a torrent of muddy yellow water hurtling over rocks.

Louder I played, and faster. Everything the rats wanted was right in the center of that river, waiting for them. All they had to do was reach for it.

They poured past me without hesitation, rabid with desire. I cringed backward from the passage of their sharp nails and whipping tails, but I kept the music going, loud and sharp enough to be heard above the roar of the river. Would the ocean of rats never end? My arms were trembling, aching from holding the pipe in place for so many hours, and my breath came short—bursts of desperate notes instead of long chains of pure melody. I played until the last line of rats arrived—the injured ones, the sick ones, the young rats clinging to their mother's sides, the old rats scarcely able to move. They all passed into the flood, and were tossed and smashed against rocks, dunked and drowned by the rushing water.

Shaking, I collapsed on the riverbank. I dared not drink the river water, not after it had swallowed such foul creatures; but I sucked in great ragged lungfuls of air, and I massaged my quivering fingers.

Dorothea arrived moments later, in the company of a few dozen children. They all carried nests of infant rats too young to follow the music on their own. Each nest was tossed into the river as well.

"The music made them squeak and squeal so loudly, we were able to find them all." Dorothea sat down beside me. "Are you all right?"

I tried to speak, but I could only wheeze through my parched throat.

Dorothea signaled to a girl, the water carrier I had met the day before. "Bring our savior some water," she said, and the girl ran eagerly to obey.

Along the road crept a few score of Hamelin's adults, peering tentatively here and there as if they expected rats to leap from the grain fields and bite them. In the lead was the owner of the inn, her leather tunic flapping against her thighs and her dark braid bouncing over her shoulder. "Well, well," she said, with the same smirk she had worn the previous night. "The Pied Piper has saved the town, it would seem. I am interested in buying your magical pipe."

"The pipe works only for me," I rasped.

"How convenient. And I suppose, when the rats return, we'll have to hire you again? And you'll take even more of our gold?"

The water girl came running back with a bucket, and I drank before answering. "They should not return for a long time," I said. "Meanwhile, you should examine your way of life. Changes must be made if you want to avoid a recurrence of the problem."

"So you admit that your solution isn't permanent?"

"I never said it was." I lurched to my feet, swaying, and Dorothea braced me with her shoulder. "Now, I must walk the town and the fields one more time to root out any stragglers, and then I will collect my reward."

"You will indeed." The innkeeper's smile was anything but reassuring.

Dorothea and some of the children accompanied me on my second scouring of the town and the surrounding fields. My music gathered up another thirty rats, which I led to the river and drowned. By that time, my ankle was paining me so much I could barely stand, let alone walk. One of the boys who accompanied us had a pair of wooden crutches; he insisted I use one of them for a while. I protested, but Dorothea jostled my elbow. "Let him do this for you," she whispered. "He is grateful. They all are."

So I accepted the loan and hobbled into the Burgomeister's home on the borrowed crutch.

He was awaiting me in his study, with the innkeeper at his side.

"I have cleared the town of rats, as we bargained," I told him.

"And you look a good deal worse for wear." He exchanged a chuckle with the innkeeper. "So you claim to have destroyed every last rat?"

"Yes, I have."

The Burgomeister clucked his tongue. "Then what do you make of these?" And he opened a box on his desk, revealing three fat rats.

My mouth opened, but I could not speak.

"You did not get rid of every single rat." The Burgomeister shook his head, as though greatly disappointed. "And the ones you destroyed were lured away through trickery and magic. Who's to say you could not magically call them back again, and charge us more money? In fact, the good people of Hamelin believe that *you* summoned the rat infestation in the first place, so you could drain our fair town of its hard-earned coin."

"That's an outright lie." My face heated, but my body was so weak I could do nothing but stand helpless.

"Fifty guilders I gave you," said the Burgomeister. "And you'll not get not another coin."

"This is blatant injustice," I said. "You're going back on your word."

"Ah, but you failed to fulfill the bargain." The Burgomeister closed up the box again. "A man of business should look more closely and pay more attention to details, or he may suffer loss of profit. Off with you, now."

Gritting my teeth, I stood tall. Never had I been more tempted to use my real magic; but the laws of my sojourn forbid such indulgence. "I will not go until you have settled the debt between us. You have accused me falsely and insulted me deeply. If you do not pay me now, you will regret it for generations to come."

The fell darkness in my tone must have registered with the Burgomeister and the innkeeper—their smirks disappeared, and they glanced at each other.

"Perhaps we could offer you something else to make up the balance? A child, perhaps? I have a good worker of fourteen years in my kitchens—you could have her. Take her along to carry your belongings, fetch things, or warm your bed."

Fury and revulsion roiled in my gut. "Your offer disgusts me."

"Ah, you would prefer a boy? You can have your pick. The innkeeper has several who would do—"

I spun on my heel and clumped out of the room with my borrowed crutch.

The Burgomeister shouted after me. "Children are cheap and good here. Well-trained. You'd be a fool to refuse."

"Then I am a fool!" I shouted back.

Propping myself on my crutch, I kicked the front door of the Burgomeister's house shut as hard as I could with my good foot. The very rafters shook with the force of my anger.

Dorothea came alongside me, her brow seamed with worry. "What happened?"

"He refused to pay me."

"I'm so sorry. These people are a covetous, tight-fisted lot."

"He offered me a *child*, Dorothea. A girl of fourteen. Of course I said no. But I'm not done with this place. They cannot cheat one such as I and not be punished for it."

"What will you do?" she whispered.

"I do not yet know. I am angry, and weary, and the day is nearly done. Might I trouble you for a room for one more night?"

"The innkeeper won't harbor you again," said Dorothea. "But I will sneak you in the back way. You can sleep with me. In my room, I mean. As we did last night."

"As we did last night," I repeated, slowly. Where she stood, in the street, the glow of the setting sun sparkled in her black curls and touched her rich brown skin, turning it to gold. I had never seen anyone so beautiful, not even in Faerie—and it was not only a beauty of face and form, but of heart. Her spirit shone with a magic beyond my comprehension. I could spend a lifetime basking in that light.

"We should go now," she murmured. "And once you're settled, I'll return the crutch to its owner. I can find something else for you to use tomorrow."

"My ankle will be healed by tomorrow," I assured her. "Faeries heal faster than humans."

Once I was settled on Dorothea's bed again, I began turning over plans for vengeance in my mind. I could summon a plague of locusts or spiders or flies. I could introduce a horde of badgers or a murder of crows to the town. I could lure in a couple of wild bears to tear buildings apart.

But any of those things would harm the children of Hamelin, and they had suffered enough. If only I could spare the young ones, yet punish the adults. If only I could create a better life for these children—

And then an idea dawned, bright and clear, in my mind.

They had offered me a child as the balance of the debt. If they would so readily part with one child, perhaps they deserved to lose them all.

It was the perfect solution. With one beautiful song I could take the laborers from these fools, so they would be forced to do their own work. If any of them did still love their children, the pain of the loss might stimulate them to change their ways, to live better lives.

As for the children, they would come with me to Faerie, where rooms and resources were boundless. Their lives would be infinitely better, and longer, too.

The Faerie elders might protest an influx of human children, but I could point to the days when we took in changelings, foundlings, and orphans. That history should serve as sufficient precedent, and my sister and my parents would support me once I told my tale. And it was time to return home anyway—this night marked the anniversary of my arrival in the human realm.

I stretched out on Dorothea's bed. I should get a few hours' sleep, especially if I would be playing tonight—but I could not dispel the whirlwind of possibilities and plans in my mind.

Children gathered outside Dorothea's room, grateful and eager, begging me to tell the tale of the rats, to explain my magic. I sat up and indulged them, scanning their small bright faces, asking their names. By the time Dorothea returned, late in the evening, she had to pick her way through a tumble of small bodies who had fallen asleep where they were,

in the hallway, without fear of gnawing mouths
or scrabbling nails.

"I have plotted my revenge," I whispered,
accepting the bread and meat she passed to me.
The meat was tough and stringy—probably
leftover rat roast, but I was so hungry I did not
care. I told her my plan between bites. "I will
play a song so high and soft that only the
children can hear it. You are full-grown, so it
will not affect you. But I want you to come with
us, to Faerie."

"Come with you? To Faerie? But—what
would I do there?"

"You can help us care for the youngest of
the human children. And you—you could be—"

"Yes?" The word seemed to hover on her
full lips, a question that must be kissed away.

Sinking my fingers into her hair, I crushed
my mouth to hers, no quiet kiss this time, a
bruising one full of wicked promises. She gave
a surprised little sigh and cupped my face in
both her hands, kissing me back with an

urgency that set my heart jumping and heated my skin.

When we broke apart, my thoughts took a moment to settle back into place.

"Yes," she said thoughtfully, with a half-smile. "I think I will come with you."

I kissed her again, quick and fierce. "Hurry then, and gather your things. We must do this in the dead of night, when most of the townspeople are asleep."

An hour later, in that frozen quiet just after midnight, I stepped from the inn and set my pipe to my lips again. I was still exhausted, and my ankle ached as I walked; but a bright clarity of purpose sustained me, lent strength to my tired fingers and buoyed my breath.

I thought of the children in other towns—helping with housework, yes, but playing, too—ruffling dogs' ears and chasing each other around the pasture. The children of Hamelin deserved that blessing—to learn, and laugh, and be loved. They deserved full bellies and safe beds.

The song I played for them was sunlight and soft breezes, green meadows flecked with flowers, limpid streams for wading and gnarled trees for climbing. It was wonder and wisdom, waiting to be discovered; it was laughter laced with freedom. The notes fluttered, high and light, slipping between shutters and ducking under doors.

From every house along the street the children came, dark figures carrying candles or lanterns. They moved slowly, burdened by toil and exhaustion. The older ones carried the little ones on their backs or in their arms as they followed me. From street to street we went, and from house to house, drawing more children to our company. A ragged band we were, a patchwork garment stitched together with the melody of hope.

At one house, the door opened and a thin figure called out to me. "Piper! Oh Piper, please!"

I approached the child, still playing, and saw that it was the boy who had lent me his crutch.

"I was late to my work because I spent time with you and Dorothea," he said. "My father broke my crutches in half so I could not go anywhere else. But I want to follow you. Please don't leave me!"

Dorothea appeared at my elbow. Somehow she was always there when I needed her most. "I will carry you," she told the boy. She took him on her back, gripped his legs to keep him secure, and trudged beside me while I played. Sidelong I glanced at them—at Dorothea's set jaw and determined eyes, and at the boy's thin frame, all bones and skin. That would soon be mended; I would provide these little mortals with all the fine feasting they could desire.

Dorothea knew all the children in town, and she told me when we had gathered every last one. Together we trooped out of the cold, dark streets, along the road through fields waving silver under the moon.

Up into the hills I led them, still piping, still weaving dreams of sparkling golden trees strung with plump blue fruit, and of vines twining around the columns of Faerie homes, and of endless gardens, tiered and towering, rich with butterflies and dragonflies and friendly sprites.

Our destination was the highest hill outside the town. I had seen a circle of white stones there, near a smooth rock face, so I knew there was a nexus at which I could make the portal to Faerie. But halfway to the top of the hill, I heard a cacophony of shouts from the valley.

I gathered the children around me, and I stopped playing. They looked anxious, lost without the music, but when I smiled at them, their frowns dissolved.

"Would you like to see Faerieland?" I asked them.

"Was that the place in your song?" asked the water-carrier girl. "Are you from Faerieland?"

"Yes, to both questions," I replied. "I'd like to take you there, if you'll allow me. I promise you will be safe and well-cared for."

"I have seen Faerieland already, in dreams," said the boy on Dorothea's back. "And I think I have always belonged there. Can your magic fix my legs?"

"Perhaps," I told him. "But Faerie favors always come at a price. And it shall be your choice. I think you are wonderful just as you are."

The boy nodded, and Dorothea's eyes glowed approvingly into mine.

The bellows and shrieks of the bereft townsfolk floated to my ears, wafting up the hillside. The sounds filled a dark, vindictive hollow within me, and I smiled again, cruel and wild. The children smiled back, small feral grins. They would fit in very well in Faerie.

"Come, my dears," I said. "We must run."

Once we reached the hilltop, it was the work of a moment to adjust the circle of stones and speak the spell. A crack opened in the rock face—a split between the realms, revealing a lush sweep of grass with a glittering sapphire lake beyond. The children bounded through, one after another, needing no music to compel them. Dorothea hesitated a moment, but she took a long look at me, and smiled, and stepped over the threshold with the boy on her back.

I followed them, but I did not close the portal. Not yet.

I waited until I could see the Burgomeister and the innkeeper struggling up the hill, accompanied by wailing townspeople. Scabbards bristled at the men's belts, and some of the women's eyes were red from weeping. For a moment I thought they resembled the rats I had drowned, red-eyed with long hairy tails.

"May you drown in your sorrow and your regret," I called to them. "The deal is done."

Then I swept my hands together and closed the portal.

4

THE HUNGRY GRASS

The body on the floor was becoming a problem.

Donovan had killed Andrea half an hour ago, and since then her muscles had relaxed, allowing the contents of her bowels to pass. He should have dragged her to the tub immediately, but he'd been too shaken to do it. Instead he'd sat down with a bottle of Dead

Rabbit Irish whiskey and numbed himself down to the bone. He was feeling warm and wiggly inside now, but the glow of the alcohol through his muscles couldn't prevent the stench of Andrea's post-mortem eliminations from slithering into his nose, sickening him. If he wasn't careful, he'd throw up the liquor he'd managed to swallow, and then he'd have to deal with his deed without any liquid buffer between him and the truth.

He set the heavy glass rim of the bottle to his lips and glugged again, then thunked the bottle onto the table and rose. The room swayed a little, but he was fine. He could handle this. There was a broad lawn around the house, a good fifteen acres. Lucky for him Andrea had suggested they move out here, to the countryside beyond the densely packed suburbs of Atlanta, Georgia. He'd been reluctant at first—not much to see or do in the country, a good thirty minutes to drive before they could get anywhere fun.

Life with Andrea was always fun. Monster truck rallies, rodeos, rock concerts, karaoke at roadside bars, random drives to the beach, hikes in the mountains. She was constantly coming up with new ideas, new schemes, new locations to check out. He had been sucked into the dizzying whirl of life with her. He'd loved the ever-changing kaleidoscope of one-night friends with whom they drank and shouted and laughed. He'd loved the frantic five-minute hookups in public restrooms, the humid makeout sessions in the back of her Honda. Not in high school, college, or the two years since graduation had he met anyone remotely like her.

And now she was leaking liquid excrement and piss onto the dark gleaming hardwood of their first home as a married couple.

Everyone had said two months was too quick. He'd proposed after one month, and they took another month to plan the wedding. In the old days people might have assumed a "shotgun wedding" or whatever the hell that was—but Andrea was careful about pregnancy. No surprise babies for her. She was having too much fun with life.

Donovan sank back into the chair and croaked a sob.

He had to pull it together.

He'd dig the hole first, then come back for her. Put her in. Cover her dented-in face with clods of dirt. Pack the soil down. Tomorrow he could go down to the Country Boys garden store and buy some plants to put in, to disguise the grave site.

No one around here knew them yet. First night in the new house. They hadn't met any of the neighbors, if there were any neighbors.

No one he knew would miss her. He'd had no one to tell about the wedding anyway, except his dementia-stricken grandfather. His dad was off god-knew-where and had been for ten years. Mother gone, breast cancer. Andrea had relatives, so she said, but none of them had come to the little wedding in the rented park pavilion. The only guests had been a few friends they'd made the week before—a couple from bowling, and a guy they'd done karaoke with, and a handful of other random acquaintances. Andrea was always making friends, new friends everywhere, all the time. She had no old friends that he knew of.

Maybe he should have questioned her about that, and about her relatives. Then he'd know who might come looking for her.

First things first—he must get her into the ground. Did they even own a shovel? Maybe the previous owners of the place had one out in the garage—it looked like the sort of garage that might hold anything and everything from decades of family life, and from the glimpse he'd gotten earlier that day, the former owners hadn't cleaned anything out when they left. There certainly hadn't been any room inside to park the Honda.

Donovan shuffled out onto the porch, into the singing summer night thick with indigo darkness, winking with intermittent fireflies. The grass stretched away from the front walk and driveway in two great wings of motionless green, each blade of grass a tiny feather.

He'd come outside barefoot, forgotten his shoes. No matter. He padded across the flaky boards of the porch, down the steps, across the pavement, still faintly warm from the heat of the day. The garage doors stood wide, the way he and Andrea had left them earlier when they realized there was no possibility of parking the car inside.

Donovan's foot crunched on something smooth-shelled and crisp and wriggling. Sucking in a breath, he jumped back, and a roach as big as his palm scuttled away. He could still feel its phantom carapace under his foot, even as he walked into the garage and found the switch for the single bulb overhead.

With a skittering scurry of prickly feet, a hundred shiny black carapaces scuttled away into cracks and corners, hiding deep in the mound of junk. The garage was packed floor to ceiling in an upswept jumble of storage tubs and children's toys, the kind made of hard rounded plastic and dyed in obnoxious primary colors.

Who would leave so much of their stuff behind? Again he wondered about the family who'd lived here before. He and Andrea had never met them. The place was a foreclosure, and much of the process had been handled virtually, including their tour. No one had staged it, but when they arrived today they'd found a few pieces of old furniture and some dishes in the cupboards. A half-full roll of toilet paper in the bathroom. A few towels, threadbare from use. No bed frames, just a bare mattress and beside it a leather shoe that looked as if it had been gnawed, and not by any animal, either. The bite marks were in a neat half-circle, distinguishably human, and too large for a child's mouth. Donovan hadn't wanted to think about what kind of adult would gnaw on a leather shoe, or why. He'd expected Andrea to laugh about it, make some sort of joke—but she'd begun acting different by then, jumpy and anxious. She'd barely looked at the shoe.

Donovan stepped further into the garage, gingerly fumbling with a miscellaneous tangle of garden tools—a few rakes, a broken snow shovel, a spade. He grabbed the spade and jerked it free, dislodging another flurry of roaches. Great. Just what he needed—a pest problem, on top of everything else.

As if being forced to kill his wife wasn't enough.

He turned, and there was a *man*. Standing on the grass beside the drivway, peering at him with pinprick eyes from dark hollow sockets, head cocked and scant lank hair fluttering in the night breeze. He was wretchedly thin and nearly naked, his papery yellow skin sucked to his breastbone and ribs, collarbones jutting out like rebar. With every breath the man's stomach caved in dramatically. A pair of ragged boxers hung from the bony ledges of his hips, and his skeletal legs ended in wretchedly thin feet.

"Spare some cash?" wheezed the man. "Bit of food?"

Donovan would have said yes, if not for the body on the floor. "Can't, sorry," he said. "I'm kinda busy." He hurried past the man, his fingers knotted painfully tight around the handle of the spade. "Look, I don't have anything to give you. We just moved here, you see, and we haven't stocked the fridge yet, and we don't have cash."

"Anything," moaned the man. "So hungry."

Donovan flinched. "There's gotta be a shelter near here. Somewhere you can go? A fast-food garbage bin you can dig through?"

Movement near the Honda caught his eye—another figure emerging. A child, probably five or so. Just as gaunt as the man, with enormous mournful eyes in a fragile white face, just tiny pale bones and bits of skin. Donovan shuddered. "Hey man, is that your kid?"

"Hungry," whispered the child, drifting forward. Donovan thought it might have been a girl. She wore a pair of mint-green panties and nothing else. As she stumbled forward, Donovan backed up, shifting the spade into both hands. His first impulse was to call the police, or Child Protective Services. But he couldn't have official types nosing around because of the oozing lump that used to be Andrea.

"You need to go," he said hoarsely to the man and the child. "Leave my property. And man, you need to take better care of your kid."

"I gave her all the food." The man's voice was a thin whine. "Lost my job in the COVID, couldn't pay bills for months. Cellphone broken, landline cut off, power and water cut off, and then I got sick, so sick, no one but her around. Couldn't call anyone, couldn't drive. I heard her crying and crying. Told her to eat the food, all the food, not much left. I tried to eat my shoes. Then she tried to eat me." He lifted his arm, showing a seeping red bite mark. "Then it was over, for both of us."

"You—you tried to eat your shoe?" Donovan could barely form words. "Wait—did you live here? In this house?"

"Our house," mewed the girl. "You took our house."

"Bought it, after it was foreclosed on," said Donovan defensively. "Now I don't know what you want, but I can't help you. Try going down the road and asking the neighbors."

The thin man's cracked lips pulled back, showed disease-darkened gums and yellow teeth. "No neighbors. No help. No one to hear."

Donovan swallowed hard against the acidic lump rising in his throat.

"Give us food," moaned the child.

"Last chance," murmured the thin man.

In Donovan's duffel bag, the one upstairs in the bedroom, there were a couple granola bars and a pack of peanuts. But if he went to get them, these two might wander around, might peep through windows, might see the body on the floor. He couldn't risk it.

"Now look here." Donovan brandished the shovel. "Get off my property, or else."

The man and the girl recoiled, clinging to each other with fingers like fragile twigs. "We'll go," said the thin man. "Fair warning, one foul turn deserves another."

"Okay, whatever." Donovan shook his head, incredulous. Who talked that way? Nobody.

The man and the girl shuffled off across the lawn; but before they had gone half a dozen paces the child turned around, and gave

Donovan a hideous grin. Her whisper floated to him like the night breeze, like a dark moth, like a curse. "Touch not the *féar gortach*."

"The *what* now?" Donovan breathed, but the girl tucked her hand into her father's and both of them trailed away across the grass, into the whispering dark.

With a shaking hand, Donovan pulled out his phone. The words *féar gortach* sounded distantly familiar, like a sickening kind of déjà vu, like a nightmare you can't remember but can still feel writhing inside you.

"*Féar gortach*—Irish myth—hungry grass?" he muttered, staring at his phone screen. According to Google, *féar gortach* was cursed grass that would sap a person's strength and make them insatiably hungry, forever. It sprouted when someone died traumatically from deprivation.

He looked up at the flat expanse of the yard, bathed yellow in the circle of porchlight, fading to gray and then black beyond. Far across the lawn, starlight touched the tips of the grass with silver. And though the realtor hadn't spoken of lawn care service, the grass was perfectly uniform in height, two-and-a-half inches precisely, if Donovan had to guess. The night breeze sifted across his own cheeks, ruffling his loose wavy hair, but not a single leaf shifted in that entire crisp carpet.

Donovan glanced back at his phone. There was another meaning to the words *fear gortach*—the thin man, or hungry man, a perpetually starved type of Unseelie ghost that begged for alms. To the generous he granted blessings, and to the stingy he brought all manner of dreadful luck.

The feeling of déjà vu made sense now—Donovan guessed that Grandpa McCarthy must have told him the story once. Grandpa McCarthy was fond of the old Irish tales—well, perhaps *fond* wasn't the word. He always told them grimly, like someone discharging an unpleasant duty. "Beware the *lianhan sidhe* and their wiles," he'd say. "Look out for men who always wear hats—they're probably pookas with filed horns. If you see a man who's short, hairy, and unusually strong, don't make him angry. That'll be a fenodyree, and they're not to be fucked with."

Donovan swept a hand over his eyes and pinched the bridge of his nose. He blinked and shook his head. Too much whiskey. Killing Andrea had taken its toll on his mind, and he'd had a strange waking nightmare, that was all.

Renewing his grip on the shovel, Donovan strode boldly onto the lawn, circling the house to the back. The grass stretched away into the dark, nearly as far as he could see, though he could make out the shadowy bulging line of the forest in the distance.

He walked far into the backyard, until the bulb by the back door of the house looked small when he turned around. Good thing he'd switched on both the front and back lights when they arrived. He was always the logical one, the practical one, the one who restrained Andrea when she got too deal. He wasn't sure how she'd made it through life so far without him, honestly.

Donovan set the tip of the spade against the turf, jammed his bare heel against the shovel's top edge, and pushed.

The spade bit down, slicing through grass blades and cutting into the root system. But this root system was particularly tough and thick, layered with thatch, because no matter how hard he pushed Donovan couldn't break through it. He lifted the spade and jammed it down again, with all his might. A few more roots popped and snapped beneath the blade, but he couldn't make the tip sink any deeper.

Again and again he tried, different spots with the same result, until he collapsed, sweating and weak, tears pulsing at the corners of his eyes.

He had to get through this damned grass, down to the dirt. Had to dig a hole to put

Andrea in, because the alternative was wrapping her in a tarp and driving her to the nearest lake, and he wasn't about to put that seeping mess into the car. He'd never get the smell out of the trunk.

He'd rest a minute, and try digging again.

With a shaking hand he tossed sweat-damp hair off his forehead. His stomach churned, growling faintly.

Donovan pressed a hand to his belly with a short laugh. He and Andrea and their friends had gone out to eat after the wedding, but he'd been so excited he couldn't manage more than a few mouthfuls. He and Andrea had planned to order dinner from DoorDash or Grubhub tonight—or at least, that's what *he'd* been planning. Andrea had had other ideas. He shuddered.

After what he'd seen with her, why did the idea of *fear gortach* seem so illogical? If Andrea was possible, anything was possible, right? Literally any *thing*. Any creature, monster, beast of the night, fell Fae presence.

He felt the prickle of the grass against his palms, and his stomach surged again, growling louder. He should get something to eat, maybe the peanuts and granola bars from his backpack—although now that he thought about them, they seemed woefully inadequate. A scant drop in the cavernous pit of his hunger.

Donovan hauled himself upright, leaning on the shovel. His muscles had gone limp and tremulous as overcooked noodles, and the aching hollow of his stomach lurched from hungry to queasy. If he did not eat, right that minute, he was sure he would throw up.

He staggered forward several paces, and then a dozen more—but the light by the back door didn't seem to draw any nearer.

Faster he walked, clutching his stomach with one hand and his spade with the other.

And still the distance between him and the light remained the same. The lawn seemed to bend and bow and sway and swell—a watery, shifting perspective, yet all the while every blade stood rigid and stone-still, immoveable.

Nausea tore through Donovan's stomach. He dropped the spade, leaned over, and retched, spilling watery whiskey and bile onto the ground.

He felt better for a half a second—and then much, much worse. He vomited again, falling to his knees in the mess, stomach sucking and heaving until there was nothing left, and he could only spit sour flecks. The dark was closing in around him, never-ending grass at two-and-a-half inches tall precisely, as far as he could see. The light of the house was only a pinprick now, like an unattainable star.

Donovan writhed toward it on his belly, sweating and shaking, too weak to stand.

If only Andrea were still alive. He could have yelled for her, and she would have helped him.

Maybe he should have let her do what she wanted to do to him. Relenting and agreeing to her plan would have been better than *this*. She hadn't wanted to kill him—only to feed from him every so often.

He'd always thought blood-drinkers had to be undead. But Andrea had a pulse, and breath, and a normal digestive system. When her fangs had popped out, slick and white, he'd panicked. He wouldn't listen to her. "I am *dearg-due*," she said. "It's a kind of Fae—we're not dangerous, not if we're fed regularly. I just need a reliable blood source, not these skeezy people from random bars. You're Irish by blood—your grandfather tells the old stories—I thought you would understand. We're married now, anyway, we can work something out—"

He'd sworn loudly, repeatedly, to cover up her shouted pleas, and then he'd picked up the poker from beside the fireplace and shoved it through her face.

It had been a bold, abrupt move, and for a moment he'd felt powerful. Donovan the Vampire Slayer, the monster-killer.

Andrea had swayed, eyes and mouth slack, drool dripping from her fangs. Then she had toppled over, and something had cracked inside Donovan. He had gone straight for the bottle of Dead Rabbit whiskey. They'd been saving it to celebrate tonight.

But as Donovan drank it, he hadn't felt guilty, oh no. Because when you find a real live monster, and it threatens to drink your blood, you fucking kill it. End of story. The moment he discovered what Andrea was, his love drained away, like rainwater through soil. Like snapping fingers—gone. And then there was nothing for it but to end her, before she could hurt him or someone else. When he plunged the poker between her eyes, felt the bone snap and the spiked end pierce brain matter, it had been oddly satisfying—as if a hunger he never knew he had was finally satiated.

Donovan shook his head to clear his thoughts. He had to focus on *this*, his immediate problem. He drew a deep breath and a few blades of grass sucked into his mouth, tasting of rain and dirt and something metallic, like old blood. Maybe it was only the taste of his own vomit. He spat, but couldn't get the grass off his tongue—it seemed to cluster and multiply, a thick thatch filling his mouth. A scream swelled inside him, but there was no outlet for it, and no air to breathe, because the grass had clotted in his nostrils, prickling out of them like Grandpa McCarthy's nose hairs.

He reached out, fumbling blindly with one hand, and sank his fingers clawlike into the grass, pulling himself forward. He was weak now, so weak, and choking, asphyxiating— Maybe if he had turned and run for the house the minute he felt the hunger, it wouldn't have dragged him down. Maybe if he'd brought a snack along—maybe, maybe—

He lifted his head a little, peering over sharp tips toward the house, but there was no house. Nothing but a broad sweep of starlit turf, even when he craned his neck and looked around in every direction. He was alone on a planet covered entirely with grass, a speck of flesh under a sky of heartless stars.

His head grew too heavy to hold up, and he dropped it like a stone into the grass, *through* the grass—his face sank between the blades and through the thatch, and he was rushing down, down, through endless twisty gnarls of root, his body shriveling because the grass was alive, and it was sucking him away, drinking his blood and draining his fat and gulping down his muscles, turning him so thin he could twist and wriggle easily between the knots of root. He sank through miles of choking earth and *roots roots roots* that filled up his mouth and ears and coiled around his eyeballs.

And then he popped out again, and he was lying on his back on his lawn, under the stars.

The hunger was still with him, but it was bigger than him now, a vast roaring need that encompassed all.

He rose, trembling, and stared down at his body. Where he'd been toned and trim, he was now emaciated, a jangling collection of bones tied together with tendons and seamed with crackling skin. He wore nothing but his underwear. Passing a quivering bony hand over his scalp, he found only a few stray locks left.

The thin man and the girl came to him out of the dark, their jointed toes pressing the grass. "Welcome, brother," said the man, and the girl shook her head and said softly, "I warned you."

"Andrea," croaked Donovan. "I have to bury Andrea."

He shuffled hurriedly across the lawn. He could move now, quite easily, and he hobbled and hopped toward the back door, his bones clunking together.

But when he stretched out his foot to the concrete step, a shock raced over him, and he was thrown back.

"Only the grass," whined the thin man. "We can only step on the grass."

Donovan tried again, and was repulsed again. He groaned, limping along the grass beside the house until he reached the front. He could not step on the front path, or the driveway, or the porch. But if he stood right beside the porch, and rose on his toe-bones, he could see through the front window a little. There was Andrea's body, slumped on the floor, growing colder and stiffer by the minute. Even with the poker sticking through her face she looked beautiful, so curvy and thick and luscious and delicious.

And Donovan thought, if he could take just one mouthful of her flesh, he would be happy forever. She would have let him have a bite, to keep him alive, because she loved him. She would have given him anything.

A spark of regret singed his brain—maybe he shouldn't have killed her—but the spark died, submerged in the endless torrent of hunger.

5

THE
KELPIE

The kelpie had not eaten in weeks.

His stomach shrank against his backbone with every rattling breath, his nostrils flaring just above the water. He had risen from the depths out of necessity, to breathe after hours of submersion—but also to check the shoreline, to see if by chance any unwary humans had approached the edge of the lake.

The water glimmered, blue and peaceful, bordered by shale and sand and sun-warmed rocks. Beyond it the trees rose, branches prickling against the sky, misted with the soft green of spring. The biting chill of winter would soon dissolve and the air would shimmer with heat, luring humans from the cities to the cool embrace of the mountains. The humans would be soft and weak from sitting in their cozy homes all winter. He thought of his massive teeth sinking into sweet, plump flesh, and shivered.

But it was still too early in the year for anyone to be wandering the edge of the lake. He'd had to leave its waters to secure his last meal—a runaway from the prison beyond the mountain. The kelpie did not care much for humans and their laws, but he saw the man crouched by a campfire, leering at images of young human girls—little more than children— and he felt a certain satisfaction in clamping his jaws over the man's throat. There were some creatures too foul to be allowed to breathe.

Sometimes the kelpie wondered if he was one of those creatures.

He pushed his narrow head further through the gleaming film of the water, until most of his neck cleared the liquid edge. His legs paced beneath the surface, keeping him afloat. Droplets clung to his long lashes, and he shook them off, with a fierce whinny that echoed off the mountainside and bounced from one side of the lake to the other. It was a cry of hunger, mostly, but also threaded within it was the ache to confirm to himself that he still existed, that the weeks down in the dark bowels of the lake had not erased him. That he had not faded into silt and bubbles and shadow.

The sound turned his stomach sour, because yes, he might be alive, but as usual, he was irrevocably alone.

It didn't used to matter so much. After all he'd been alone for years, since his sire and dam died. They were old, with centuries of wisdom to guide them, and they told him that life in remote places was best for creatures like them—old servants of ancient Celtic gods with no place in this world of satellites and cell phones and swarms of jabbering humans.

So even after their carcasses rotted at the bottom of the lake, he stayed where he'd been born.

He should visit their bones again soon, he thought. It had been too long since he paid his respects.

Slowly he swam toward the shore, his nostrils flaring, picking out scents of damp earth and fresh leaf buds, new grass and delicate violets sprouting in mossy hollows between the trees.

His hooves struck pebbles and he clambered out of the lake onto a narrow strip of beach. He shuddered all over, shaking the water off his slick black coat, and flicked his tail so a shower of sparkling drops arced through the air. He stood there, chuffing and breathing, trying not to think about the ravening emptiness in his shrunken belly, or the way his ribs jutted through his skin. Soon he would be too weak to hunt, and then he would be an assembly of bones and skin, drifting slowly through murky purple depths to join his dam and sire in their eternal rest.

The water streaming off him had soaked and dappled the sandy shale under his hooves. He pawed at the damp ground, raking up a crumbled seam of mud. Should he stay in horse form for hunting, or switch to human form? Humans generally responded better to a horse than a strange man, especially a naked one. He could wear a set of clothes from the chest he kept under a rock nearby—but the clothes usually didn't help set humans at ease. Too damp and dirty, too full of centipedes, smelling too strongly of mildew, maybe.

Before he could make up his mind, he caught a strange scent—a fragrance that sent a sickening bolt of hunger straight through him. His ears pricked forward, catching the rustle and creak of bare twigs a moment before the human girl stepped out of the forest.

She was slim and pale, purple shadows painted under her eyes—but she had enough flesh on her bones to last him for a few weeks.

He bowed his head, overcome with tremulous gratitude—the urge to worship her, or whatever kind power had sent her to him, to save his life.

She stepped forward, hand outstretched, apparently taking his bowed head as an indication of friendliness. A half-sob, half-laugh escaped her. "I *did* hear a horse. I thought I was going crazy—but here you are. You're beautiful, aren't you? Beautiful, and—" Her fingers floated over his muzzle, not quite touching him. He saw the change in her expression as she noticed his teeth, so large they could never be hidden beneath his lips, the way a normal horse's teeth could. "Beautiful," she repeated. "And savage. What are you?"

He'd been asked that question before, and he hated it. He'd learned to bite through his prey's vocal chords before they could speak it. But for the first time in his thirty years of life, he wanted to answer, to speak his truth to someone.

His truth. How could he speak it if he didn't know it himself?

What are you?

He snorted, shaking his head and backing a step away from her.

He should end it now, snake his long neck forward and snap, biting through tendons and cartilage and arteries. His teeth, powerful as they were, would make quick work of that soft little neck of hers.

Or he could do what his ancestors used to do—tempt her onto his back, swim her out into the middle of the lake and drag her down, down—introduce her to the family. A dark laugh bubbled inside him as he pictured pulling her to the bottom of the lake, her eyes frozen wide, her body limp and lifeless—*Hello Mother, Father*, he'd say. *I'd like you to meet my latest catch.*

The girl hesitated, her eyes wary, and then something changed in her gaze—a kind of desperate recklessness flaring to life. She stepped boldly forward and laid her hand on his nose. "I don't really care what you are," she said. "You're *someone*. And I need someone right now."

He stilled under her hand, the smell of warm, tantalizing flesh flooding his nostrils, heightening that ravenous hunger in his gut. Was she insane? She could tell he was dangerous, that he was *Other*, and she didn't care?

He nearly tossed his head and bit her hand off. It would be easy, like snapping a branch in two. The work of a moment. He could imagine the bones crunching to powder between his powerful jaws, the fingers slipping down his throat one by one. The scent of the blood, its tang on his tongue.

But part of him wondered, with a sick delight, how long he could hold himself back. And so he did not bite her immediately, but waited.

The girl's hand traveled along his face, to his broad cheek. She rubbed his damp neck, twisted her fingers through his mane, and began absently to flip the strands back and forth, working them into tiny braids while he stood silent and breathing, and holding his hunger in check.

"I'm lost," she said. "Or maybe I ran away. Is that a thing, getting lost on purpose? If it is, that's what I've done. I was with a group—some stupid survival thing. I thought it would make me feel more alive."

She laughed, as if it was the most ridiculous misunderstanding in the world, and the kelpie's skin shuddered at that trickle of sound.

"I can't shake it, you see. The feeling that I'm sleepwalking through my life, that I'm never really awake. I can't really get close to anyone, and I've tried—believe me. I'm just—out of sync with the rest of them. I'm the piece that doesn't fit." She patted his shoulder. "What about you? Do you live out here all by yourself?"

He huffed in answer, and shifted his weight.

"I see. Too savage for the rest of the little common horses. Too much of the devil in you, right?" She raked her fingers through his mane again, and a twinge of pain shot through the roots. He clicked his teeth, a sharp warning, and she stroked his cheek. "Sorry. Such tangles here. Wish I had a comb."

She kept talking, murmuring to him about her family, and her roommates, and a million small human things that he didn't understand, had no context for. He tried. He knew bits and pieces about human life. But mostly he gathered the vague impression that she was alone, like him, and that she felt herself worthless, with no higher purpose besides consumption, no meaning beyond the empty cycle of the duties expected of her.

At some point he grew too weak to stand any longer, and his legs folded under him; and still he did not rip a chunk out of her slim warm arm, or bite through her jeans into the rich thigh-meat there.

When he lay down, she sat against his flank, collecting bits of shale in her fingers and flicking them into the rippling lake.

"I'm lucky," she said earnestly. "Others have it so much worse. But I can't shake the feeling that my very existence is pointless."

The kelpie thought he could give her a purpose. Consuming her life would sustain his. But would that really be any use? What was he but a mythical monster of hate and hunger? Perhaps they were both useless to the world.

He sighed deeply, and the girl leaned across his back, resting her head on him. He arched his neck and looked at her with one eye. Her face pleased him, though he had no idea if other humans would think her beautiful. He liked the slow blink of her lashes, the creaminess of her skin, like morning clouds, and the bronze shimmer of her hair. The ache of his hunger had faded a little, but it was still there, gnawing.

He would have to eat her soon. But first, he would watch her a little longer, because it seemed that she was falling asleep.

The girl had not felt peaceful for weeks.

When she pictured her soul, it was a frail, strained thing, pulled tight and fraying at the edges, worn so thin she was afraid it might disappear.

Sometimes she wanted to disappear.

Sometimes she feared annihilation so deeply she thought she might scream.

When she faced the horse on the bank of the lake, and noticed the unusual size of his square teeth—hideously, warningly prominent—she thought for a moment it might be the end after all.

She thought of old stories, fanged devil horses from the deep.

The possibilities flashed through her mind, and she hesitated, poised between flight and daring.

In that moment she felt more awake, more alive than she had for a very long time. So she touched the demon horse, her skin sizzling with the knowledge that he could rip her in half in a second.

When he didn't, she pushed her luck a little further. She touched him, talked to him, unsure if he could understand, if he was even real. She'd been so torn and twisted lately, she could barely trust her own mind. But stroking the horse's damp sides as they grew drier and warmer in the spring sun soothed her suspicions. Maybe he was only a normal horse after all—lost perhaps, and incapable of understanding her words, or the soul she poured out before him.

When she ran out of words, she draped herself across his back and relaxed. Why did she feel so peaceful here, with this immense black horse whose bony sides and fierce jaws spoke of primal hunger?

Why hadn't he consumed her yet? Torn her to pieces, gulped her down, or dragged her into the lake water to be drowned and chewed apart slowly, at his leisure?

She sat up, her fingers rippling over the prominent ribs. He looked half-starved.

"You're hungry," she whispered, and his ears swiveled to catch her voice. "Why don't you eat me?"

He eyed her for a long moment. Then he opened his jaws, baring his bulging gums and massive teeth, and the long purplish tongue lying between them. Was it a yawn, or a threat? Clearly he'd shown her his teeth on purpose.

"Do you want me to leave? I could—I could get you some food, and then come back."

In answer, he flopped over onto his side, as if every bit of his strength was spent.

"You just eat meat, right?" Where on earth could she get raw meat out here? Maybe if she could find her way back to her group, she could steal some meat. Ted had brought along those sausages in his pack, carefully nested in ice— he'd be pissed if she stole them, but after his condescending attitude toward her on this trip, she didn't care. A little vengeance was totally in order.

She might be able to find the camp again, if she really tried. They were probably looking for her, anyway.

No.

This was ridiculous.

Meat-eating demon horses are not real, she told herself sternly. *You're an idiot of course, as usual.*

She sighed. "This is so dumb, right? Me thinking you're anything but a sad, lost horse. A horse who eats *grass*. Ugh, I'm such a moron."

Had she hoped it was real, that he was some kind of mythical monster? Yeah, sort of. As a kid she had always wanted magic to be real—had wished and wished and hoped that faeries and elves might really populate the woods behind the playground.

And this—this was just her own stupid desperation, her reluctance to do the adulting thing, manifesting itself in some kind of weird delusion.

She scrambled to her feet, burning with anger at herself, and with unreasonable rage at the black horse lying on the ground.

"Get up!" she snapped. "Get up, now. If you're really a water horse, show me. Eat me. Right now. Come on. You're hungry, aren't you? Starving—dying maybe—so go ahead, damn you. Take a bite!"

The horse lifted his head, his lips writhing back over his yellow teeth. Hot breath hissed from his mouth, and he heaved his bulk up, climbing to his feet, towering above her. He stood, shaking, for a moment, and then his muscles coiled and he surged up on his back legs, rearing, a sharp cry bursting from his throat.

A cry that sounded nearly human.

The horse's body changed, morphing smoothly, not painfully like the werewolves the girl had seen on TV. This was a seamless slipping from one form to another, forelegs easing into muscled arms, skin lightening to a rich brown instead of night-black—the tail disappearing and the mane rearranging into an abundance of dark hair, still retaining the tiny braids she'd woven into it.

He stood before her, bare and lean, his ribs just as painfully prominent in this form, his teeth white now, but still slightly too large for his mouth. The lower canines protruded a little, denting his upper lip.

The girl hadn't screamed when she realized his Otherness, or when he yawned so widely—but now she wanted to scream.

"It's okay," the man said, his voice scratchy from disuse. "You can scream. I'm used to it."

But the girl reminded herself how he had lain in the sun and let her tell him her troubles, without so much as raking a tooth's edge across her skin.

"What are—" she started to ask, and then she caught herself. "Do you have a name?"

"It's Brónach."

"Brónach," she said carefully, trying to mimic his pronunciation. "What does it mean?"

His mouth tightened, and he didn't answer.

"Do you have any clothes, Brónach?"

He nodded, almost eagerly. "I do. Come."

She followed him over the rocks, trying not to look below his waist. It was difficult. Thin as he was, he was nicely shaped.

He struggled with a rock near the edge of the lake, his breath coming short, and she had to help him lift the stone. Underneath, in a crevice, lay a wooden box, and inside that was a set of moldy jeans and a dirt-stained plaid shirt.

She wrinkled her nose. "These are your clothes?"

His face fell. "Are they not right?"

"No, they're fine. A little damp and dirty, but fine."

She turned away while he dressed, and racked her brain for the name of the demon water horses she'd heard of in her grandfather's old stories, back in the days when the world seemed wicked and wonderful, not the drab, sour, redundant place she now knew it to be.

Kelpies.

Yes, that was it.

"You're a kelpie," she said, whirling.

"Yes." He had shrugged on the shirt, but left it hanging unbuttoned. The effort of dressing himself had apparently winded him, and he sat down, looking away from her, out at the water.

"You are hungry," she said. "But you didn't eat me."

"I'm beginning to rethink that decision," he said, low. "I will die soon if I don't eat."

"I can get you some food, I think. But I'll have to leave now, so I can get back to my camp and then come to you before dark. You'll be all right for that long, won't you?"

"Yes. But you said you were lost."

She laughed, pressing her hand to her chest, wondering why she suddenly felt so fiercely alive, so full of purpose. Maybe it was magic.

"I'm not as lost as I thought I was," she said. "Wait here, and I'll be back."

The kelpie sat on a rock until it cooled under him. The sun ducked behind the uppermost branches of the trees, and the breeze whisked ripples across the water and chilled his bones. In human form he wasn't as impervious to the cold. He felt vulnerable, fragile, and oh so hungry.

Why had he let the girl go? He'd had meat, fresh meat, within reach, and now his meal had run off into the woods. She'd promised to return. But when had a human and a kelpie ever made a pact, and kept it? Granted, it was usually his kind doing the deception, turning traitor after promising safe passage. Still—trusting a human? What had he been thinking?

He slid from the rock into the water, seething. He'd revert to his water horse form, so he would be stronger. Strong enough, hopefully, to kill the girl when she returned. He was weak from winter starvation, but if he hid, if he caught her by surprise, he could rip into her with his teeth before she even knew what was happening.

"Brónach!"

He started, his heart leaping in his chest at the sound of his own name. He'd heard her say it twice already, but this time, spoken in this bright, expectant tone, it carried two truths that he felt in his very bones.

She had come back.

She wasn't afraid.

"Brónach?" More hesitant this time, as if she was beginning to doubt herself, to imagine that he'd been a dream. "I brought food. I'm sorry it took so long—I had trouble finding my way back here..." Her voice trailed away, and her shoulders slumped, light fading in her eyes, like the rays of the setting sun.

The absence of that light twisted into his heart like a sharp thorn. He couldn't bear it, and he rose from the water, clothes dripping, his bare feet slapping against the rocks. "I'm here."

"Oh." She exhaled, and smiled. "I thought maybe I imagined you."

He eyed the pack on her back. "What have you brought? Not that tasteless dried stuff the hikers call meat, I hope? If so, I'm afraid I'll have to eat you after all." His mouth curved up at one side as he said it, an unconscious impulse, because he was warmer inside now that she was here. Warmer, and fuller, in some place more important than his belly.

He felt her presence like a hand on his heart.

She swung the backpack to the ground and opened it. "The people I came up here with might kill me," she said. "But I brought you our sausages. We were going to cook them over a fire tonight."

"Cook them?" he exclaimed, shocked. "Why would you do such a thing?" His hand darted out, seizing the clear bag, which was packed full of meat smushed into casings. "Why ruin what is already perfect?" He slit the bag with his teeth and dug in with his fingers, capturing a fat sausage and swallowing half of it in one gulp.

The girl laughed, surprise and delight, and he grinned up at her, conscious that there was meat in his teeth, and not caring. She didn't seem to care either. She sat beside him and ate dried fruit from another bag while he inhaled the sausages one by one. They were very cold, not warm like fresh flesh, without the satisfying rip of meat and the crunch of bone, but he was too starved to mind. In this form, he was less of a predator anyway. His human shape was meant to lure prey, to draw them nearer. He'd never seen his human face clearly, only in spattered reflection in the lake water—but from the way the girl watched him, she clearly found his features appealing.

He liked her face, too. In fact, the more times he glanced at it, the harder it was to look away. He met her eyes again, and again, and it felt tentative and prophetic at once, like the first drops of rain touching the lake's surface before a downpour.

The sun was nearly gone now, its last eddies bathing the shoreline in amber light. When she glanced down, gold glinted in her lashes and along her eyelids. She looked up again, straight into his eyes, and he felt something lock into place—a channel between them, pulsing with vivid energy.

"I should go," she said, but she did not move.

"You should," he agreed, and he moved a little closer. A restless energy had possessed his fingers, his body, and he couldn't be far from her at this moment. He needed to be nearer— and even that wasn't enough.

The wind scoured across the lake and swept up the bank, and the girl shivered. He watched her bare arm, fascinated by the way the hair lifted and the skin stippled. The reaction was gone in a moment, but he touched her anyway, his fingertips gliding from her wrist to her elbow. "Are you cold?"

"A little." She was rigid, tense. Strange, because earlier in the afternoon she had stretched herself along his side and told him her stories.

"Would you be more comfortable with me if I were in my other form?" he asked.

"I like your other form." Her voice was faint, barely a breath as she leaned nearer to him. "But this one is—nice, too." Then, softer still, as her breath ghosted across his lips— "Are you going to bite me?"

He wasn't sure what was about to happen, but at the moment he felt neither famished nor savage. Pinpricks of light sparkled along his nerves, and his lips tingled, anticipating— *something*. Something new. Something special.

"I won't bite you," he whispered. "A bite would damage you, and you should be whole. You are perfect, exactly as you are. Something precious, I think. Not something to use or consume."

She leaned back, her eyes narrowing. "What about other humans? You've eaten them before."

"Yes."

"What made them different? Were they any less precious, or worthy?"

"I—I don't know. I never thought of humans as anything but prey. Until today." He didn't understand why her mood had changed, in the space of a bare second.

"You—have eaten—*people*. Torn them apart with your own teeth. And I—I was going to—" She lurched to her feet, pressing her hands to her temples. "What is *wrong* with me?"

He withdrew into himself, jaw tightening. Of course. The human had come to her senses at last. Here was the fear and disgust she should feel, the emotions he had expected when they first met.

"Can anyone know what they don't know?" he said bitterly. "Until today, I didn't know what a human could be, had never spoken to one for more than a handful of words."

"That's no excuse." She shook her head, adamant.

"I only do as I was taught. I am what I am, and I can't change it."

"Can't, or won't?"

"Would it matter? You seem determined to think of what I have done, and not what I'm doing now."

He spoke, defiant, but he cringed inside, because he wasn't sure what it would mean, to change. To do and be something else, something new. He had his rhythm of life, his favorite nooks of the lake, his forest. He had his favorite flavors of human, and he cherished each of the meals, rare as they were. He was no more or less than this. He had changed more than enough for one day—to shift his pattern any further would be dangerously akin to a rejection of his lifestyle, his parents' lifestyle, his ancestors' legacy.

The girl paced the beach, avoiding the anxious pain in his eyes, her thoughts no longer peaceful. She had operated in a kind of delighted frenzy of purpose for most of the day, but now she realized the full weight of what he was, and what he had done. It mattered, didn't it? Of course it did. A lifetime of murder could not be expunged by a moment of mercy. Her pity for him, the connection she felt—it didn't excuse his violent acts, or justify ignoring them. Did it?

"Why does it matter to you what I've done?" he said, rising to his full height, stepping in front of her and blocking her agitated tramping across the beach. The ratty open shirt he wore stank of mildew, but beneath that, she caught the scent of his skin— the essence of wild water, lakeweed and mountain air and whispers of pine.

"It matters because I'm human."

"And you are therefore responsible to hate me or punish me, on behalf of those I've killed?" He shook his head. "So why feed me then?"

"Because you spared me," she muttered.

"And that makes me deserving of life?"

"No. Maybe? I don't know—" With him this close, she couldn't think properly, couldn't sort out all the logical and moral reasons for her to hate him, to walk away, to hold herself back from the surging need to touch him, teach him, help him, step into the emptiness she could feel in his soul. Maybe she would fit there. Maybe all he needed was someone to see him, to show him another way.

"You told me you needed someone," he said softly. "That I was *someone*."

"You were a horse at the time."

He chuckled. "True. But you knew there was more, didn't you? And you didn't care. So why does it matter now? What are you afraid of?"

She grasped the folds of his shirt, looking at her hands and not at him. What did she fear? Not his teeth, or his savage nature. At the root of her reluctance coiled the fear that caring about someone like him might change *her.* Might make her a little less human, poison her with more darkness than she was prepared to take.

But she had darkness already, a thick sludgy reservoir of it, sucking her down a little deeper every day.

What if leading him out of his darkness helped her conquer her own?

His wrongs are not against you, she told herself. *It's not your place to forgive him. Maybe it's your place to help him be more than a monster. Maybe that's why you're here—*

"What are you afraid of?" he asked again, more urgently. "Me? I wouldn't kill you when I was starving, and I won't now. Not ever. Not even if you put your fingers between my teeth, not if the taste of you was all I craved—"

She yanked him closer and rose on her toes, pressing her lips to his parted ones. He tasted strangely delicious—raw and wild, sweet as mountain laurel and savage as dark water.

Whatever words he'd been about to say slipped into her mouth in a murmur of helpless wonder, and the tension of surprise faded from his shoulders, easing as he relaxed into the kiss.

The kelpie felt a dark magic in the girl's kiss, a magic that crept into his soul and untwisted what was wrong inside him. Had he feared change? It seemed a ridiculous apprehension now. Moments ago he'd shrunk from the thought of leaving the lake, of finding a way to sustain his life without harming humans.

And now, as the sky grew darker overhead, the brightest possible future unfolded in his mind. He would have to give up something, yes—the security of knowing his place and purpose. He would be free-floating in an uncertain world whose rules and habits he didn't know.

But if she were there, it would be all right. He'd never dreamed that one human could have such power, to transform the world from dreary solitude to a place worth living. That just by *existing*, a person could make the universe better.

All this burst in his mind while he kissed her back, his hand sliding up her neck to the back of her head, weaving into her hair. He felt alive, alive, *alive*. Joyful. Ready and able to do anything, his body brimming with strength.

The girl stopped kissing him, sucking in a long, wavering breath. "Wow."

He'd never heard that word, but he could guess what it meant. He grinned at her, letting the light in his heart shine through the smile.

"So you're coming with me," she said. "We'll need a cover story for you—you're a lost hiker with amnesia, maybe. You'll live at my place, and I'll buy you meat, any kind you like. You can do online school—it'll be fine. There's a park near my apartment, with a pond—maybe you can go out there at night sometimes, and swim. This will work. It's fine."

"Wait. Slow down." He cupped her face in both hands, tilting it up to his own. "I'll come with you, but first, we'll spend the night here. And I need two very important things from you."

"What things?"

"First, your name."

"Jillian. And the second thing?"

"Another kiss."

Her eyes sparkling in the evening gloom. "Um, *yes.*"

When she kissed him the second time, he felt a more powerful impulse, a deep ache to be near her, with her, part of her. He wrapped both arms around her and pulled her as close to him as he could. But he sensed that this need, like his kelpie's hunger for flesh, must be restrained, and managed. So after a moment he let her go.

Under the crisp white stars he took her hand, and swept his other arm toward the sparkling lake. "Care to go for a swim?"

She gave him a wicked half-smile. "Only if you promise to warm me up afterward."

The words, and the look that went with them, tingled through him in unexpected ways, and he caught his breath at the surge of new sensations. It was comforting to change, to revert into the form of the water horse, sleek black skin and shaggy mane, long legs and powerful muscles. He nosed against her cheek, and she stroked his muzzle.

He nudged her over to the rocks so she could step up and reach his back, and he stood still while she mounted. With a flare of his nostrils to catch the night air, and a toss of his head, he plunged into the black, star-studded lake.

Her breath hissed at the cold water submerging her legs, lapping her thighs. Her fingers tangled in his mane and her knees pressed tightly to his sides.

Further and further he swam, until they were at the very center of the lake, with the water sparkling in shades of night-blue and ebony, and the dark trees rising like swathed figures along the shoreline.

This was the spot where the kelpie would dive. Would take his victim down, down, under the surface, into the gurgling liquid world where he lived.

She would spasm and flail, her eyes wide with terror and betrayal, limbs stiff and desperate, clawing for the border between lakewater and air. He would hold her in place, jaws clamped around a leg or arm, or maybe her slim waist, until the movements ceased, and she floated, calm and impassive, forever his.

No change necessary. He could consume her, and forget this day, and go on as he'd always done, as his kind had done for countless generations.

It would be the perfect betrayal, a consummate feat of wicked deception. His parents would have been proud.

The kelpie trod water in the center of the lake.

The girl on his back waited, and her hands tightened in his mane.

"Brónach," she said.

He stirred, the spell broken—or perhaps reforged.

"I'm ready to go back to shore," she said. "Please."

The kelpie swirled through the water, aiming straight as an arrow for land, and the lake parted around him, streaming behind him in glossy ripples.

When they reached the pebbled beach, the kelpie lay down in a hollow beneath the trees, where the aroma of violets perfumed the night air. And the girl curled against him, warmed by his skin and his breath, and they slept.

In the morning he took one last swim. Disappeared under the lake's surface for so long the girl wondered if he would return.

When he resurfaced and took on human form, he said simply, "I had to say goodbye."

Then he put his hand in hers, and walked away from the lake, and from the cold bones of the water horses in the deep.

The **IMMORTAL WARRIORS** adult fantasy romance series

Jack Frost

The Gargoyle Prince

Wendy, Darling (Neverland Fae Book 1)

Captain Pan (Neverland Fae Book 2)

Hades: God of the Dead

Apollo: God of the Sun

Related Content: *The Horseman of Sleepy Hollow*

The **PANDEMIC MONSTERS** trilogy

The Vampires Will Save You

The Chimera Will Claim You

The Monster Will Rescue You

The SAVAGE SEAS books

The Teeth in the Tide

The Demons in the Deep

These Wretched Wings (A Savage Seas Universe novel)

The DARK RULERS adult fantasy romance series

Bride to the Fiend Prince

Captive of the Pirate King

Prize of the Warlord

The Warlord's Treasure

Healer to the Ash King

Pawn of the Cruel Princess

The INFERNAL CONTESTS adult fantasy romance series

Interior Design for Demons

Infernal Trials for Humans

MORE BOOKS

Lair of Thieves and Foxes (medieval French romantic fantasy/folklore retelling)

Her Dreadful Will (contemporary witchy villain romance)